ISBN: 978-1-9192637-3-1

Cover Design and Artwork - © Provoco Publishing
Reproduced under license
Individual author photographs reproduced with permission
Logo Design - © MJC at Martyn Carson Creative
Edited by Jane Murray

Not Another Christmas Anthology

The Dark Claus

By C W Grumley

She would have never volunteered if she had known what was to come. But no one knew. And that is how they intended it.

The Arctic cold bit at her skin, but the heat of the scope trained to the back of her head kept her warm. A rail rifle, set to disintegration. No witnesses. No evidence. Just the way He always wanted.

Doctor Alexandra Hale turned her deep blue eyes from the reindeer as she brushed and spied an automaton of the Santa Corps. Fluid tubes flowed from a thermal unit at the machine's back and lit its exo-armour an ominous red. Tubes spilt from beneath the bug-eyes set deep into a cold, black metal face and crawled over his shoulders towards a thermal inlet. Frost could kill a person in a matter of hours in the tundra, and even the automatons would freeze solid without sufficient thermal protection. Her eyes drew to its hands; they gripped the weapon tighter; a mechanical finger poised at the trigger.

'Point that thing away from me,' grumbled Hale, pulling down the dense winter hood of her jacket and freeing her mouth from beneath a balaclava. Wisps of golden hair tickled her face as winds from the Arctic storm raced through the opened stable door.

'Quiet slave!' snapped the automaton, his voice warped and synthetic. Snow crunched beneath its feet as it strode inside the reindeer stable and crashed the butt of the rifle across her face.

A warm trickle fell from her nose, which froze before it made her lips. She peeled it off before the frostbite took hold. Hale glared upwards.

'Get back to work.' The machine turned promptly and returned to his station at the enclosure entrance.

What was the point of fighting? There was none. Some had

tried to flee over the years. They had even made it several miles from the compound. But no one ever made it off the Arctic ice sheet. Either the Santa Corps got you, or the frigid temperatures did. The lucky ones were mauled by the polar bears that prowled the outermost perimeter of the compound. Quick deaths. Not slow and harsh. It was a sickening feeling, but Hale had long resided herself to the fact that, once they had you, the only way out was death by one means or another. But she was in no mood to die, at least, not yet.

Biting her lip, Hale replaced her hood and mask then returned to the reindeer. She brushed again, then set it down and reached for the syringe gun and an ampoule of fluorescent yellow vitamin serum.

'Arsehole,' mumbled Hale. The reindeer cocked his head. Deep brown eyes, heavy and sullen, stared at her. She did not know why, but she loved Blitzen the most. It was as though he could read her... somehow, in tune with her emotions. She had not felt a connection to anyone or anything since Kerim had escaped. He had volunteered with her and seven others several seasons ago. But one night a few years ago, he disappeared... just like the others had. The official line from the Corps was that he had been tracked North of the compound, and then the trail went cold. As they always did, the Corps concluded that he was dead somewhere out on the ice sheet. Bitterness suddenly filled her as she thought; he had left her alone in a frozen hell at the top of the world.

Hale looked away from the reindeer and tried to push the memories of Kerim away. Though she tried to convince herself that he did not matter, she could not escape the truth: she had loved him and missed him deeply. And with the others having tried to escape over the years, she was the last remaining soul besides Him, His wretched automatons, and the elves. Her face sank.

Restless hooves stomped the hay-strewn pen. Hale met the creature's despairing gaze. Collecting herself, she stroked his side and patted his rump.

'Ignore me,' she sobbed, then wiped her running nose. 'Right, boy. This'll sting… it always does.' The doctor pressed the syringe barrel to Blitzen's rear. A blasting hiss filled the air, then a deep growling complaint from the reindeer as the serum disappeared. Hale rubbed the area, calming her friend as she did.

A thin voice suddenly broke the howling winds of the tundra. It grew louder and more panicked as it neared.

'Doctor Hale! Doctor Hale!'

The doctor stood, and the automaton turned. They stared towards the faint lights of Santa's village, barely visible through the whiteout. Slowly, a small figure grew into focus. It was the elf and close friend, Alabaster Snowball, but what was so urgent he risked his life racing across the compound without a guard entourage. His explosive collar clunked on the jingling bells around the neck of his uniform as he ran.

'Halt!' exclaimed the machine. The tubes pulsed with red fluid. 'Where is your escort?'

'I-I—'

'Speak!' The machine raised his weapon. The barrel charged, glowing ice blue.

'I… the Doctor… she… we… there's been an, erm, accident, I—' The rubbery, pale skin surrounding Alabaster's deep black eyes loosened. The nostrils of his sharp nose flared with fear.

'Reasoning denied. Primary punishment, death.' Its voice became ever more distorted. Alabaster shrank. His voice vanished. He trembled terribly as the rail rifle chimed its full charge. 'By Claus decree…'

The elf closed his eyes.

A piercing bolt of blue energy pierced the night sky, searing a hole through the dense cloud overhead. The machine turned, crashing its weapon across Hale's face. She collapsed to the floor, face stinging from the pain and blasting tundra winds. Mounting her, the automaton reached behind its back and pulled out a small black cylinder. With the push of a button, two prongs emerged, a bright blue energy beam suspended between them. It thrust the beam towards her neck when a voice through the storm stopped it instantly.

'Hold. Subroutine 7-6-alpha-sierra-charlie-dash-4.'

Black, lifeless bug-eyes, recessed into the polycarbon exo-armour, stared at her. Hale gazed back. Stiff and unmoving, the machine lingered over her momentarily, then a pneumatic hiss gave out, and gears in its servomotors spooled. It stood up and stepped aside.

Hale scrambled back to her feet as a tall, dark figure emerged through the driving snow. He wore a dense jacket of red and white fur with similar trousers and hat. His bushy grey beard bore icicles that clinked on his chest. Heavy black boots pounded the snow.

At least Santa doesn't lie to the world about how He looks, just everything else, Hale thought. She swept a dense collection of snow from her winter jacket before it could freeze.

'Alabaster comes on my orders without guard,' said Santa. 'I sent him ahead as he is much swifter of foot than myself.' The fat man chuckled. Hale turned her head in disgust at the sight. 'Dr. Hale.' The doctor promptly returned her attention to Santa and hoped he had not noticed her displeasure at being in his presence. 'There has been an accident, and I wish you to assess the situation before I plan my next steps. It is urgent. You will follow me without question.'

Hale stiffened, her gaze fixed on the towering presence of Santa Claus standing before her. She started a resigned shrug but stopped herself, thinking better of it. The cold nibbled at her trembling lips.

'I am your servant,' she said, bowing slightly.

Through the driving blizzard, they crossed the compound towards the training enclosure at the far side. Dim lights, set atop a low ice wall, outlined a sizable circular area beside a two-story wooden barn. Its walls were coloured red and white except for a door at its flank. It had always stood out to Hale as an anomaly; the door was new, silver and shining. Beside it, a tiny keypad glowed through the gloom. She had always wondered what lay beyond. It was the only place in the compound she had not seen in her nine seasons. None of them had. Only Santa and the elves ever seemed to go there. Once, she had tried to ask Alabaster, but he warned her about asking such things and sidestepped her question. The not-knowing chewed at her insides.

'There,' growled Santa. 'That's where the damned beast got in.'

Hale, breaking from her thoughts, peeled her gaze away from the door and looked to where Santa pointed. At one side of the yard, shattered ice outlined where something powerful had smashed through. Rushing forward, Hale followed the trail of ice chunks to a pool of blood. A dark smear of blood, mingled with paw prints, led off to the right. She ran beside the blood trail to another blood pool which surrounded the dead body of a polar bear and a stricken reindeer, lying side by side.

'Rudolph!' Hale cried, kneeling beside the reindeer. The creature grunted in pain, its precipitating breath becoming heavier and more difficult with each passing moment. Alabaster walked up beside her.

'You've got to save him, Alex,' the elf whispered.

'How,' retorted Hale under her breath. 'The aorta is severed. Nothing will save him. Oh, Rudolph.'

'Hale, if you don't save him, He'll kill me and my family. It… it… I was… he was my respons… Please! You've got to do something.'

'I can't perform miracles.'

A deep, grunting voice came over Hale's shoulder.

'Well. What is the diagnosis, Doctor?'

She struggled to restrain her disgust. Did He not care? But simultaneously, she could not deny her worry about the fate of the dying creature in front of her.

'It's fatal, Santa. The main artery has been lacerated. The only humane thing left would be to put him out of his misery.' Hale rose to her feet, wiping tears from her cheek before they could freeze.

'Well, that is a shame, and right before Christmas. I feel for all the children who will wake up with empty hearts and stockings.'

Hale, gritting her teeth, tightened the straps of her thermal coat and tucked in her gloves. *If only they all knew*, she thought. Anger threatened to consume her, but she suppressed it and swallowed hard against a dry throat. She turned to face Santa.

'How could this happen again?' Hale shook her head. 'That's at least one a year since I've been here. I thought the Corps was meant to prevent this!'

'It is the Pole, Doctor Hale… accidents happen.'

Hale bit her lip.

'Let's move on then, shall we?' Santa looked towards the automaton. 'Termination protocol Eight-pappa-bravo. Alabaster —'

The elf turned solemnly and reluctantly on his heels.

'— come with me. We have things to discuss. Doctor Hale! Return at once to the housing block. Your services are no longer required this evening.'

Santa turned and made towards the silver door at the side of the barn. Alabaster followed close behind. Every few steps, he glanced over his shoulder, casting a desperate gaze in Hale's direction. At the door, Santa punched in the keycode, and it slid sideways. Santa entered, but Alabaster cast her one last look. She looked back with apologetic eyes; she wanted to help him, but what could she do? After a long moment, the elf stepped inside.

A stiff polycarbon arm crunched into her left shoulder and sent her stumbling forward.

'Move. Housing block.' The automaton walked beside stricken reindeer, charging the rail rifle and lighting the yard an icy blue.

Hale, pausing briefly, turned and ambled away. There was nothing she could do for Rudolph now; he was moments from death. Everything seemed to go quiet for a moment. And Hale could no longer feel the cold biting her fingers, face and toes. She went numb. Suddenly, a muzzle flash illuminated the darkness, and a splitting crack reverberated into the night. Air and flesh seared with the heat of the rail bolt. A putrid stench filled her nostrils.

It was horrible and made her feel sick.

Hale rolled to her side, looked along the length of the housing block, and let her mind wander momentarily. Empty beds lay all around her, those of the other eight volunteers who had come to the Pole brimming with seasonal joy. *Why have they not sent more? Or... is this it? And I'm doomed to die alone*, she thought. The thought would burn in her mind from time to time, but then it would dissipate. And being alone for so long brought her an odd sense of comfort. It allowed her to imagine what the others would be doing had they never come here, where they would be, and what their lives would be like. She imagined them in their homes, surrounded by loved ones. Then she would think of Kerim. Would they have ever met? What sort of life might they have shared if they had? Hope would fill her, engulf and warm her like a blanket. But tonight, for all she tried to distract herself with this daydream, Hale could not shake her worry for Alabaster and the burning desire to know what was behind that door. Rolling onto her back, she stared at the frost creeping through the crack in the ceiling above her.

The door at the far end of the room creaked open. Hale sat upright and darted her eyes to the door. Peering through the gloom, she saw nothing. Startling as a hand grasped her leg, she looked to her feet and saw Alabaster standing there. Blood dribbled from his nostrils. One eye was half closed. The point of his left ear had been torn off, and flesh dangled loosely from it. Alabaster stumbled forward.

'Alex,' he whimpered.

'Alabaster! What... what has he done to you?' Her concern was palpable. She jumped off the bed, dashed to the bathroom and doused a rag with water. Rushing back, she patted his nose, smearing the blood across his top lip. Hale went to grab the loose flesh from his ear, but he batted her hand away, grasped her bed shirt and pulled her in close.

'You must get out of here,' Alabaster grumbled.

'We'll never make it. You know —'

'No! You have to go.' Alabaster released her, and Hale sat back on the low bed.

'But how? There's nothing beyond the compound boundary. It's just miles and miles of tundra. And with nothing but my thermal clothing, I wouldn't make it five miles before I froze.'

'I can help with that.' Alabaster pulled a small disc from his pocket. He depressed its centre, and the room filled with a warm, red glow.

Hale closed her eyes as a wave of warmth swaddled her like a blanket. Images flashed across her mind. She sat before a roaring fire, the flames lapping her face with heat and soft light. It was paradise. Cold suddenly engulfed her. She opened her eyes to see the room descended in gloom once more.

'Take this thermodisc. Find shelter, and it will keep you warm.'

'Where did you get that?'

'I took it… from Him.'

Hale paused momentarily, drawing her eyes over the elf, then took the thermodisc from his outstretched hand and stuffed it into the winter jacket hanging from the foot of the bed.

'He'll kill you when He finds out I've left. He'll know you helped me. What about your family?'

Conflict drew across the elf's face. Leathery eyelids closed shut, and he inhaled deeply, calming himself.

'I'm doing this for my family.' Resolve washed over him. 'But first, you must do something for me.'

Hale dropped from the bed to her knees, bringing her eye level to his.

'Anything.'

Alabaster paused. Words stuck in his throat. Hale knew she would not like what he was about to say.

'You need to tell the world what He does to the volunteers and… to us elves. But you can't just tell them —' Alabaster tensed, an almost imperceptible tightening of the shoulders, and he turned his eyes to the bleak wooden floor. Hale thought quickly, and a sudden realisation took her.

'The barn?'

Alabaster nodded without looking at her.

'You… you must… come with me.' He turned to face her. His coal-black eyes quivered as tears threatened within them. 'I've… seen things. Horrible things. Things no living creature should have to see. If the world found out, it would destroy Him; He needs to… to be… stopped.'

Hale stared at him for a moment. She knew the danger she would find herself in, but her curiosity and resolve steeled her nerves.

'I'll do it. I'll come with you. Show me the way.'

Alabaster blurted a sob. Tears began to stream from his eyes, and he wiped his nose on the sleeve of his jacket.

'Thank you, Alexandra. Come… follow me.'

Hale donned her thermals and winter jacket, dashing with Alabaster from the housing block towards the inner perimeter gate.

The Arctic night bit at her cheeks, as they slipped through the access point to the inner compound. Flicking her eyes this way and that, she ran in a crouch. Looking back, her boots dragged trails in the snow now that the wind had died. Snaking from building to building, they sneaked by the few patrolling automatons and made their way to the far side of the inner compound, towards the Southern gate. Through the other side, they raced towards the barn. Slipping and skidding across the icy ground, they slid to a halt against the ice wall surrounding the reindeer training yard.

Hale peered over the wall, sweeping her gaze all around.

Nothing. Eerie quiet hung over the training yard and the tundra beyond.

Feeling a tug at her sleeve, Hale turned and followed Alabaster up to the silver security door. A small panel protruded from the panel beside it, and the elf, reaching up on his tiptoes, thrust his hand inside a dark opening. A sweet festive melody played aloud, then the door wheezed pneumatically as it ground open, and they stepped inside.

Descending an elegant silver staircase, they went spiralling down until they came to a sublevel several stories beneath where they had entered. They emerged onto a steel platform to one side of a large cylindrical room, which plunged for several stories more. Hale scanned, spotting cryodispersers which lined the walls. Multiple frozen pipes spread from each one like frosted arteries, creating an interweaving web of piping that crawled downwards.

Hale moved from the platform to a circular walkway suspended in the centre of the room. At the railing, Hale dropped her vision down the vast shaft.

'What is this place?' she whispered, but her voice still echoed slightly.

'A laboratory. He brings us here to... to do things.' The elf paused, his grey skin paling. 'Truly horrible things. This is what we must tell the world.'

A voice suddenly boomed upwards from below. Hale knew instantly to whom the voice belonged, and she dived backwards.

'Is the serum ready?' said Santa.

'Yes, master,' came the squeaky voice of an elf.

'We do not have much time. We must begin the sequence immediately.'

Hale crept forward. Five levels below, Santa stood beside a large machine with a bright opening at its centre. A bed with loose shackles extended from it. He stared at the computer screen. Data traceries dashed across before him. His fingers danced gracefully over the screen, and the machine burst into life.

'Oh no!' blurted Alabaster.

'What!? What is it?' snapped Hale.

'It's started. We don't have much time. We must move quickly before the cycle ends.'

'What are you talking about? What cycle?'

Alabaster dashed off as he spoke.

'Quick, Alexandra. There won't be much time!'

'Wait!' Hale followed hastily after him. 'Alabaster, stop! What's -'

'He's bringing the next subject,' said the elf, panting. 'We must get the data before He can finish the cycle, or all will be

14

lost. You want to expose Him, don't you?'

Hale found new determination, settling the questions burning in her mind. She followed the elf down to the second level, where he veered off suddenly into a side room.

A vast computer screen covered the icy wall to her left. All around, clusters of consoles and heavy laboratory equipment dotted the room. Tucked in the far-right corner, a machine stood alone in a glass room, white light shining up from the floor. They moved closer, and as they did, she could see several luminous yellow vials suspended within it.

Alabaster raced forward, jumping onto the computer beside it, tapping furious fingers across the screen.

Hale meandered towards the machine and gazed at the glowing yellow serum. Realisation gripped her.

'This is the vitamin serum I give to the reindeer.' Her nerves set on edge as the elf beside her stopped dead in his seat. She turned slowly and stared at Alabaster. 'Alabaster… what is this place? What is this serum?'

The elf said nothing, then turned to face her, his eyes flooded with tears.

'The others never escaped, Alex.'

'Wha… what d'you mean they "never escaped". Are they still here?'

'I'm sorry, Hale.'

Hale's eyes widened, blood drawing from her face. The elf struck the screen with a balled fist, and the white light coming from the floor turned blood red. A siren sounded. Leaping from his seat, the elf slipped past a glass door just as it closed.

Fear gripped Hale, her heart pounding through her chest. She smashed a balled fist against the glass. She begged Alabaster to let her go, but the elf stood still, a silent wreck of a creature staring back.

Hale crumpled to her knees, sobbing, screaming. She cursed the elf and herself for being led into this situation. Then, she suddenly drew silent.

'Good work, Alabaster.'

Santa stood over the elf, staring down at her.

'Let me go! Let me go!' demanded Hale. 'You can't do this. You can't —'

He choked back the amusement beckoning at the back of his throat. 'My dear Dr. Hale, you are mine. You declared as such in the contract you signed when you volunteered for this post. As such, I own the right to do what I wish with you, including what I am about to do.'

Panic replaced fear. Hale felt her breathing shallow, the air thinning with each passing moment. She leered at the pathetic and defeated form of Alabaster Snow. He outstretched a hand and pressed it to the glass, mouthing his apologies. Anger filled her, and, for a moment, images of violence crossed her mind, and then a gentle hissing filled her ears. She spun around and saw nothing, but her legs began to feel heavy, and her vision spun. She stumbled forward, collapsing onto the machine. Clinging to it, she could do nothing as the strength in her arms failed, and she slid down to the ground, and she felt consciousness leave her.

What's happened to me? she thought.

A foggy haze lifted from her eyes as she roused. Looking around, she made out the thin metal bars of a pen and wooden walls. Shifting her weight, the raking scratch of straw irritated her skin. She stretched an arm forward, touching the frigid steel of the cage, then slipped. Confusion filled her as she spied the palm of her hand... only it was not a hand. It was nothing like a hand but a hoof instead. Hale pinched her eyes closed.

It's all a dream... a bizarre dream.

But the image before her eyes would not go away. A hoof hung where her hand should have been, and instead of an arm, it was a long, thin leg covered in dense white fur.

What the hell?

Stunned, Hale recoiled. Shooting backwards, she hit the wooden wall behind her. Pain spread through her back, and she cried out a dull grunt. Hale jerked again, a thrash. She tried to speak. A grunt again.

What's... what's happening, where am, what am...

Across from her, Blitzen rose his hooves onto the top of the pen. He grunted terribly, then paused, gazing with a longing stare.

Hale tried to collect herself. She trotted forward, gazing hazily at the reindeer across from her. Concentrating as best she could, she looked him up and down, then peered into his eyes. Something came to her, and it sent a chill down her spine.

No. No. It... it can't be... Kerim!?

His eyes confirmed her suspicions.

Nausea rushed through her. She dashed to the frozen water trough in the corner. Horror filled her at the image reflecting from the glass-like ice. Heavy boots thudded on the wooden floor behind her. She eased her gaze around.

Saint Nicholas, dressed in a bright red suit trimmed in white and a broad black belt at his waist, beamed a grotesque smile at Hale. Brown leather gloves strained as he squeezed the bars of her pen. He chuckled as he replaced a red and white hat.

'Time to fly, Hale. These presents won't deliver themselves,' said Santa, chuckling as he spoke.

Her nose began to tickle. Then, a red glow suddenly filled Hale's eyes. She could not believe it.

'You will guide my sleigh tonight.'

Christopher Grumley's first sci -fi fantasy duology is due for release in 2026 /7 and will be available from Amazon and selected retailers worldwide.

Mr. Havelock

By John F. Howard

"Oh, just give me a break!" Caleb shouted out loud despite being completely alone in the back garden. His mother's latest rant about how useless teenagers are, and how all they do is cause their parents nothing but angst and heartache, was still ringing in his ears as he paced round the rectangular lawn that was bordered by an array of colourful flowers that she loved and cherished more than him. A sudden urge swept over him to destroy the flowerbeds. *"That would teach her,"* came the malicious thought as he bitterly pondered another three days of Mum's house arrest, a punishment for suspension from school. Sweat ran down his brow as the burning midday sun beat down on him as he made his way to the patio, an area that played host to reasonably comfortable garden furniture and, more importantly, shade. He elected not to go through with his flower execution; Mum would probably have him arrested!

Making himself as comfortable as possible on the grey chair, which was part of a Rattan Cube dining set, another thing his mum seemed to appreciate more than her son, he placed his feet on the glass table and smiled knowing full well that the woman that had given birth to him would be apoplectic at the sight of his dirty sliders making their mark on the matching glass table. It wasn't that he wanted to annoy her, but Caleb was becoming increasingly tired of being her emotional punch bag. Christian had escaped, finally getting his own place and his own life. *"Not that my precious older brother can do any wrong!"* Caleb's thought saw his face take on a snarl as resentment rose inside him. He loved his sibling, but he'd not been here during the bad times, when his father had announced that twenty-four years of marriage no longer meant anything to him, or at least not as much as his blonde secretary, who was probably of similar age to the union with his wife. But somehow, his dad's pathetic lust and midlife crisis was the fault of the one male who'd not gone anywhere. No wonder he enjoyed the odd joint!

That, of course, wasn't the view of the school, who felt their punishment of a week's suspension was more than fair, considering the "severity" of the offence. The loss of mobile phone and the grounding was an added sanction courtesy of his mum.

"I am just so sorry, Mr. Waterford," Caleb could still hear her pitiful voice as she sat in his Head of Year's office full of shame and embarrassment. *"He's never done anything like this before."* Her eyes filling with tears did bring contrition out of Caleb, who took no pleasure out of seeing her upset. Mr Waterford, on the other hand, was a different matter. His dark, thinning hair, sharply parted to the right sat on top of a face that wore an expression that made you believe he'd smelt dogshit before he spoke to you, and housed a tone that let each and every pupil of Hillside Secondary that ever crossed his path know that he saw you as scum and believed you were always likely to be so. Caleb's Head of Year was only missing a small, dark moustache and then the comparison would have been completely obvious.

"Have you nothing to say for yourself, Dawson?" Waterford hissed in Caleb's direction. *"I would have thought you'd have known better, although I suspect the company you keep may well have something to do with it."*

"Because Leo is unfortunate enough to be in care, Sir?" Caleb's answer drew the ire of Waterford as his mother displayed an expression that was a mixture of horror and anger as she looked at her son. Mrs. Dawson knew he was a bright boy but was also a young man who was not the best at knowing when to keep his mouth shut, a facility he could have done with at this specific moment.

"Caleb!" His mother blurted out.

"That's quite alright, Mrs. Dawson," Waterford seamlessly went from patronising sleazeball to mendacious politician as his gaze

moved from mother to son. *"It is of no interest to me that your friend is a looked after child, but it is my concern if two of this school's students are bringing, and using, drugs on school grounds."* He rose from his chair and leaned on his mahogany desk which, of course, was impeccably arranged and reflective of his obsessive nature, and tried to look intimidating. *"Now I suggest you remove that monstrous chip from your shoulder and focus on your education and future. You have been predicted good grades in your GCSEs, Dawson, you have the rest of your life to look cool, or whatever word your generation uses as you continue to butcher the English language."*

"Well, it certainly isn't 'cool'," Caleb managed to keep this thought in his head, although his mother knew her son was on the verge of saying something that would probably result in expulsion and knew full well that she needed to get him out of this office.

"Quite so, Mr. Waterford," Mrs Dawson began, *"I shall keep an eye on him and make sure he learns his lesson."*

"I don't doubt it for one minute, Mrs. Dawson, he's not a bad lad and I can clearly see he comes from a good family." Caleb was already out the door as his mother and his pompous prick of a teacher shook hands. He tore off his tie and was thankful that Waterford's office was a small walk along the corridor to the main entrance and exit. Slamming the door open with enough force to rattle the frame, he let out a deep breath and perused the car park till his eyes found the Ford Mondeo which he presumed would be his lift home. His mother was not far behind and heard the noise his exit made.

"What exactly are you playing at, Caleb?"

"Which bit, Mum?"

"Well let's start with your attitude towards Mr. Waterford."

"Oh, the sleazy snob that looks down his nose at everyone, especially those that have to live with other kids they never chose to live with in a house ran by strangers, all because one parent died and the other is a crackhead!" Caleb vented as he needed to purge his feelings.

"Mr Waterford was not suggesting anyth..."

"Yes, he was, Mum!" Caleb cut her off. *"How many times has Leo been in ours? Has he ever stolen anything? Caused any trouble? We both*

smoked the weed, I'm as much to blame as he is." Caleb gritted his teeth and pointed towards his Head of Year's office as his face went crimson. "But all he sees is a 'Care Kid', the fucking arsehole!"

"Enough, Caleb!" Mrs. Dawson's voice wasn't raised but her son knew that tone well enough to realise that she was done with this conversation. Letting out a sigh, she moved towards Caleb, who now towered her by at least five inches. "I've nothing against Leo, he is welcome in our home any time, but smoking cannabis is wrong and, not to mention, illegal." Caleb's eyes met hers as his heart pounded slightly less. The sudden gust of wind was welcome as he tried to cool down. "I am not an addict, or a dealer, I just needed something to mellow me out." Caleb was fighting back tears; he wouldn't admit it, but his father's departure and Christian flying the nest had hurt him, and he knew full well that his mother wasn't coping anywhere near as well as she was making out.

"It is no excuse, Son, this can be the start of a rocky road into addiction or worse, and you will be in the house until your suspension is up," Mrs. Dawson held out her hand, "and I will have your phone."

Although house arrest and giving up his beloved mobile had angered Caleb, it was the hypocrisy that had really reignited his rage. He was trying to let his mum know he was struggling and all she could do was kick him while he was down. "And what about your addiction?"

"Excuse me?" Her son's question had taken Mrs. Dawson by surprise.

"I put the bins out, Mother," Caleb's tone was laced with anger. "I'm not blind, I see the empties. Just because the Pinot Grigio comes from Booths doesn't mean you can't get addicted to it as well."

"Don't speak to me like that, Caleb," Mrs. Dawson was defensive as well as stern in her manner.

"Like what? The truth hurts and your hypocrisy is unreal," Caleb's composure was once again lost. "No matter how many bottles of wine you sink every night it won't change the fact that Dad shagged his secretary!"

This was the first time that either of Caleb's parents had hit him and his mum, despite being of slight build, delivered a perfectly placed slap across her son's cheek with considerable force, although his adrenaline had taken care of the pain for now. Reaching into his pocket, he handed his phone to his mother, who now had tears streaming down her face. Mrs. Dawson took the electronic device with a shaky hand as her son turned away from her.

"*Caleb…*" she began.

"*I'll walk home.*"

"*But… son…*"

"*I said, I will walk home.*" Caleb tenderly touched his cheek as he stormed off.

The unmistakable sound of Dennis' yapping brought Caleb back to the present, sweltering day. The family Dachshund, who had Mrs. Dawson to thank for his name, looked at Caleb with a gaze that could have meant anything from wanting food to simply demanding attention. Tan in colour rather than the more traditional black with smidgens of brown, this mini four-legged force of nature was Caleb's only source of company, other than his mother, as he saw out his sentence. Leo, who had also received the same suspension as Caleb, would be subject to a 'consequence' which was his care home's word for punishment and usually resulted in a loss of independence meaning he, too, was not allowed out. Meanwhile Christian was too busy with life for his younger brother and Dad had his new interest. Picking up Dennis, he instantly felt the little fella's powerful tail slapping his bare legs as he resisted his slobbery advances. Placing the dog down again, Caleb had a quick scout of the surroundings and located the little plastic ball that enthralled Dennis but drove his mum insane, hence why the chewed-up, plastic sphere was outside. He picked himself up, collected the dog's source of immense amusement and threw it down the garden while he watched as the two-year-old canine set off like a missile to retrieve it, before manoeuvring his prized possession around the lawn with his nose. He'd already fallen foul of Mrs. Dawson on a number of occasions by damaging her roses, but Caleb preferred that rather than being licked to death. He pondered taking him for a walk but then remembered that he was grounded. *"Can't have it both ways, Mum!"* The thought made him smile as he turned and headed to the house for a cold refreshment, nearly tripping over the ball-obsessed Dennis, who had an unerring ability of getting under the feet of the humans with incredible speed have seemingly been at the other end of the garden not twenty seconds ago.

"Watch it!" Caleb scolded the dog as he booted the plastic ball down the driveway which was the opposite direction of the garden and led to the main road. Dennis didn't mind and enthusiastically set off to retrieve his bounty, with no sense of danger as he disappeared from sight. Realising that the dog would quite happily tackle a main road without a care, Caleb set off after him. The last thing he needed was anything to happen to the dog, something that would probably send his mum under. Darting onto the driveway, he caught sight of Dennis and the tall, dark figure that seemed to be engaging with him. His mouth suddenly became drier than ever, and his sweat was now cold as the day took a darker turn. Thoughts of unease and fear swept through him as a macabre notion was embodied in a figure who was mere inches from the family pet.

"Dennis!" Caleb shouted, although it was a rarity the dog ever listened. Today, however, was an exception and the Dachshund bolted back to Caleb as quickly as possible, minus the ball. Caleb collected him in his arms and could feel his body shaking as he let out a whimper. He looked up, transfixed by the dark figure, who made his way down the driveway and headed straight for them. Purposeful in pace but not rushing, the more detailed image of an elderly man came into view. Dressed in a black suit and tie, he looked around seventy-five and was paler than anyone Caleb had ever seen. His eyes were dark and bore into the teenager, whose heart began to race, as he held a shaking and distressed Dennis as the man stood about two feet from them. His hair was a thick, silver mane that was neatly combed back off his grey forehead and Caleb couldn't help but think about how the temperature had suddenly become a lot cooler, despite the intense rays of sunshine. Reaching into his pocket, the gentleman pulled out Dennis' ball and extended his arm.

"Pardon the intrusion, young man," he spoke like a Shakespearian actor. "I assume this belongs to your little friend, there?" Caleb's mouth was dry as he clung to Dennis, who was still shaking and in no mood to leave his arms.

"Erm… yes, it is," Caleb reached out an arm and took the ball from the elderly gentleman as he tried to clear his throat. He was thankful that Dennis was both small and light as he was now holding him with just one arm.

"Thank you." Caleb's nerves were making him thirstier than the heat ever had, which made him so much more uncomfortable and awkward. The gentleman that stood before him was polite, charming but unsettling.

"I'm Mr. Havelock," the stranger introduced himself. "He's a delightful little fellow but doesn't appear to be too fond of me."

"He's not great with strangers," Caleb's attempts not to sound nervous weren't working and he had the distinct impression that Mr. Havelock knew it.

"Understandable," Mr. Havelock replied. "I suppose you have told him to not speak to strangers." Although he appeared to be making a joke, his expression remained the same. He barely moved his thin lips as he spoke and his intense stare was eerie and unsettling, and made Caleb even more desperate for him to leave, though the teen was unsure just how to do it. How he wished he had a bit of weed on him!

"Well, thanks again for bringing his ball back, please don't let me keep you." Caleb felt he'd done a good job with instigating Mr. Havelock's departure.

"How old is he?" Mr. Havelock had seemingly not taken the young man's hint or had just ignored it.

"Erm, he's two." Caleb licked his lips as this gentleman gave him an overwhelming sense of foreboding.

"You don't sound very sure." Mr. Havelock's comment

irked the boy who felt a sudden rush of anger and bravery rise inside him.

"Well, he is two and I am sure," Caleb attempt to hide his irritation behind a smile was futile. One negative emotion had replaced the other as his unease made way for ire. Perhaps this was that thing Leo spoke about, flight or fight mode.

"Have I said something to upset you, young man?" Mr. Havelock's tone and expression remained the same, everything about this man rang alarm bells for the young man, who was done with small talk.

"No, but I have things to do and must be getting on, so, can you please leave?" Caleb turned and headed back for the patio and into the house through the patio doors, with Dennis still holding onto his human companion for dear life. Turning the latch to lock the door behind him, Caleb took a deep breath before negotiating the kitchen and heading into the lounge, which had a perfect view of the front gate where he hoped Mr. Havelock would be heading towards.

And sure enough, the slender, dark figure of the man who had made both Caleb and Dennis feel so uneasy strolled rigidly towards the main road, turning just as he made it onto the pavement to take a look at the Dawson residence. Fearful of catching his gaze, Caleb dived down below the windowsill, instantly feeling stupid but also relieved that he was no longer in the company of the creepy gentleman who seemingly affected both temperature and atmosphere. Slowly rising high enough to peek out the window, he saw no sign of him as Dennis suddenly regained his bravery and began barking furiously at a figure he could no longer see.

Caleb let out a sigh of relief and stroked the dog's tiny head, "You certainly showed him, Dennis," he said with a wry smile.

Mrs. Dawson wore a look of shock she made no attempt to hide when her pale son bolted out of the house to help bring the weekly shop inside. Roles were reversed as child grilled mum on where they had been. She'd answered her son's questions with an amused smile but was somewhat bewildered by Caleb's sudden change in attitude as unhelpful thoughts slowly invaded her head, as she began to suspect the worst. Delving into the often malignant minefield that was the internet, her mothering instincts had gone into overdrive upon reading the horrific tales of paranoia and extreme changes in personality that comes from smoking cannabis, and was driving her to levels of distraction and distrust that were only eased by a glass of wine, which she knew was worrying the son she was so concerned about. But Caleb's mother was determined to believe her glass was always half full and happily accepted her son's helpful gesture and felt a great sense of contentment upon choosing to make his favourite for dinner. She took a deep breath and allowed herself a positive moment of pride upon watching her son put the shopping away but was crestfallen upon seeing her son's lukewarm response to hearing the news that she was making chicken and sesame seeds, a Chinese concoction that was his favourite and the most perfect of peace offerings.

Sitting down to dinner, her son's mood had changed. Mrs. Dawson began letting out exasperated sighs as her son pushed food around his plate with his face facing downwards. Caleb had gone from a chatty bundle of nervous energy to a sullen teen that communicated in grunts in a mere thirty minutes. Dennis seemed his usual self, tail wagging as he employed the wide-eyed cuteness ploy in order to sample some of the dish Caleb seemed disinterested in, as his doggy bowl in the corner of the kitchen remained full. Eyeing her son, Mrs. Dawson placed her knife and fork onto her plate, which provided the desired effect of attracting his attention. He quickly raised his eyes and looked at his mum shaking her head quickly as though she almost had a twitch, as he continued to meet her gaze.

"Well?"

"It is very nice," he said, as he continued to think about Mr. Havelock, a figure who made his blood run cold.

"I could believe that if I actually saw you taste a morsel," Mrs. Dawson let out another deep sigh. "Is this because of your phone, you know -"

"It has nothing to do with the phone," Caleb interrupted with a raised voice as his knife clanged to the floor, much to the delight of Dennis, who quickly went to investigate. Caleb moved the Dachshund away before retrieving the item of cutlery from the shining tiles. Using the dinner table as support, he pulled himself back to his seated position and found his mum still looking in his direction.

"What?" Caleb asked in a defensive manner.

"It isn't your phone; it isn't the food that is 'very nice', but you haven't touched. So, what is it?"

"What is *what*?"

"You helped me with the shopping, talked the leg off me, and I'm grateful, but then I make your favourite, and you can barely look at or speak to me." Mrs. Dawson bit her lip and glanced over at the wine fridge. "I am sorry I hit you but…"

"It isn't you." Caleb raised both hands as he cut his mum off again. Breathing heavily, he pondered what to say next.

"Well, what is it, then?" Mrs. Dawson's tone was more like a plea. "It's not drugs, is it? Do you owe someone money?"

"Someone came to the house before," Caleb said bluntly as he rolled his tongue around his lips nervously.

"Who?" Mrs. Dawson replied before having a drink of water and wished it was something stronger thanks to the thoughts now running around her brain.

"I've no idea," Caleb began. "Dennis chased his ball down the drive and by the time I got there a man was trying to give it him back." Now Caleb quenched his thirst with his fizzy drink, before letting out a small burp as he covered his mouth. His breathing slowed and his stomach felt lighter as he suddenly sensed a twinge of hunger. He picked up his fork but was distracted by the smile that was now being worn on his mother's face. He remained motionless and waited for her to explain herself.

"And that's what has been bothering you," she said, with a slight chuckle.

"You didn't meet him, Mum." Caleb replied briskly as he began to blush.

"I apologise, son," Mrs. Dawson tried to clear her throat, "I was just worried, that was all." She reached out and stroked her son's arm softly. "I do love you, Caleb."

"I love you too, Mum," he said quietly, as he realised that he was now ravenous and needed to make up for lost time with his evening meal. Picking up his cutlery, he began to eat quickly, his peripheral vision enjoying his mum's loving gaze as Dennis now assumed a more relaxed pose as he continued to track the dinner progress. Both mother and son smiled and gave slight chuckles before Caleb broke the silence.

"Mr. Havelock was creepy, though," he looked pleased at his own assessment of today's caller but stopped immediately upon hearing the clattering of the knife and fork and the screech of the moving dining chair. His mother was wide eyed and pale.

"What did you say?"

"That he was, erm… creepy."

"The name, Caleb."

"Mr. Havelock," came the reply. "That's what he said his name was. Do you know him?"

"I really don't appreciate your joke," Mrs Dawson rose quickly and took her plate to the bin.

"What are you on about," Caleb said, his face scrunched with confusion. "I'm not joking, a man came down our driveway today and introduced himself as Mr. Havelock."

Mrs Dawson threw her plate into the sink before yanking open a kitchen drawer. Her frantic search soon located a corkscrew which was quickly introduced to a bottle of white wine.

"Mum, what is going on?" Caleb was now on his feet. "I'm not lying. I -"

"Mr. Havelock is dead!" snapped his mother, who was now decorating her glass with a healthy measure. "So, either this is some sick joke, or you are like the boy in the *Sixth Sense*!"

John F. Howard's debut novel, A Scandal of Secrets is currently available from Amazon and selected retailers worldwide.

Hooked On Love

By Dawn Treacher

Life can get a bit dull once you're over fifty and who wants to date a middle-aged woman whose cardy is covered in cat hairs. Well, love had long since lost its attraction, one messy divorce saw to that. And that's probably how life would have stayed, if it wasn't for crochet.

Now don't go thinking crochet is just for old ladies who sit around hooking endless scarves for charity stalls. Crafting has never been so trendy. Old is the new vintage; second hand is retro and re-using old wool which you've unravelled from a moth-eaten cardigan is saving the planet and as such is super trendy.

Even my old caravan parked out the back can suddenly be called retro-chic, especially since it's no longer road worthy. The seat cushions sag and the kitchen cupboards are wonky. For me it's a place to hang out and escape my teenager's dreadful taste in music. Camped out here with a glass of wine and my latest crochet creation, I could be anywhere. My two cats, Bramble and Motley, rather think it is theirs and who could blame them. It's a tiny slice of peace and tranquillity in the not so salubrious back streets of Crompton and it was here that my life was about to change.

I could easily fit half a dozen people in the caravan and if my neighbour wasn't pulling my leg, people would pay good money to learn to crochet. So, I put an advertisement in the local Gazette, and "Hooked on Crochet" was born, or so I hoped.

My friend, Muriel was the only one to reply to my advert.

"Maggie, no one reads the local paper anymore. Haven't you heard of social media?"

"Of course I have." That's all Abbie ever does these days, a Snapchat obsessive, I think they call it."

"Let's leave that to the teenagers," said Muriel. "Facebook, now that's more our age group. Get Abbie to create a group and post it on the "What's on" pages."

Muriel may as well have been talking in a foreign language, and I doubted Abbie would find the time. It's not exactly cool to help your mum make a public embarrassment of yourself. But much to my surprise she agreed.

"You need a name, Mum. No, you can't just put a crochet group. How about Hookers?"

"Absolutely not," I said. "I'm not looking for perverts. It makes me sound like a prostitute."

"Hooked On Crochet then, that sounds pretty catchy."

So, Hooked on Crochet it was and much to my surprise I soon had three people asking to join.

"Charge them at least a tenner a session," said Abbie. "And more if they want you to provide the wool."

"I thought tea and biscuits might be nice."

Mum, get real. Offer Pimms or Prosecco, that's what my mate's mums drink, so best make it more like fifteen pounds a session."

As it turned out milky coffee and Bourbon biscuits were the more the ticket as Brian turned out to be an octogenarian and Candice and Morag would soon be applying for bus passes. But it was a great first night. I added fairy lights round the windows.

"What made you want to learn crochet, Brian?"

He was surprisingly sprightly for over eighty and he insisted on kissing me on both cheeks before he sat down.

"Life's much too quiet," said Brian, dunking his Bourbon. "And you can't beat a bit of female company," he winked.

Candice and Morag knew more gossip than the columnist of the Sun and kept us entertained with local scandal until Abbie banged on the caravan door.

"A late addition," she called. "This is Louisa."

Brian lost count of his stitches and dropped his crochet hook on his lap. Louisa, her peroxide perm tumbling over her shoulders, leaned over to shake his hand. Poor Brian didn't know where to look.

"Come and sit with us," called Morag. "Brian's crochet is already rather wonky; we can't have you distracting him."

Morag and Candice shuffled over to let Louisa squeeze her generous bottom down and introductions started all over again. I was relieved to find that none of them were absolute beginners and that I found myself making coffee rather than trying to show them how to do a treble crochet in a granny square. Shame really, as I'd been looking forward to seeing if I had what it took to be a teacher. By the end of the evening, Brian had at least six inches of a scarf and Candice and Morag had steadily hooked enough squares to make half a cushion. But Louisa, well I'm not sure crochet came naturally.

"I was tired of being teased down the pub," said Louisa. "You know the sort, all beer bellies and loud farts. They reckon blonde barmaids have nothing up top but their tits. Well, I reckon there's more to me than a pretty face."

Candice choked on her coffee and Morag nudged her friend's arm.

"What about you Maggie," said Brian. "What made you start this group?"

"Not likely to find a second husband here," laughed Candice.

"I'm not looking for love," I said.

"Who said anything about love," said Morag. "We all need a little of the other."

I rounded up the empty mugs and carried them to the sink.

"I hope you make it next time."

"Definitely," said Brian, kissing Morag and Candice on the cheek. He buttoned up his jacket and left, but not before letting Louisa plant a big kiss on his cheek.

"Well, how did it go?" said Abbie. She was uploading pictures to our Facebook group; ones she'd made sure I'd taken during the evening.

"I enjoyed it," I said, and I meant it. I wasn't sure it was what I'd expected but it had left me feeling needed and that wasn't an emotion I felt much anymore. Abbie had stopped needing me at seventeen and that only left Bracken and Motley and frankly they were indifferent to me except for mealtimes and that was purely cupboard love.

"Should you be posting those pictures?"

"Everyone does these days, Mum. The more the better."

Wednesday evenings became a day I looked forward to. Brian's scarf grew longer; Candice and Morag finished a pair of cushions and debated whether to make some bunting for my caravan and Louisa finally crocheted a square. And me? I wondered about what Morag had said. Brian loved to talk about his late wife, and I realised that even before our divorce I had never really loved Abbie's father. The only memories I had left were of arguments over who was going to do the dishes and why could he never find time to take Abbie out. Louisa's life seemed to be an endless stream of dates that she'd met through dating sites, and I couldn't even remember the last time I'd been out with a man, let alone taken one home with me.

It was our fourth meeting when Louisa brought someone with her.

"I hope you don't mind Maggie; I've brought Michael with me." Behind her stood a man in his early thirties, all dark hair and never-ending legs and eyes I daren't look at.

"He's my little brother and that bitch of a girlfriend has finally kicked him out. I couldn't leave him alone at my place eating beans on toast now, could I? You don't mind, do you?"

Considering Michael was already sitting squashed between Candice and Morag and Bramble had curled up on his lap what I thought was irrelevant.

"Ooh, wait till I tell Georgina that I sat next to a dish like you," giggled Candice.

"How do you like the older lady?" teased Morag. "A little bit of experience goes a long way you know."

"Morag!" I felt decidedly hot all of a sudden and pushed open the caravan window.

"At last, another man," said Brian, shaking Michael's hand. "What are you going to crochet?"

They all looked at me, and I was sure I was blushing, and it had nothing to do with the menopause which had yet to rear its ugly head.

"How about a granny square?" said Candice. She piled balls of wool on the table and handed Michael a hook.

"Bit tricky don't you think," said Morag.

Michael looked at me. "I like a challenge, why not, bring it on. Who's going to show me?"

"Maggie of course," said Louisa, pulling Michael out of the clutches of Morag and Candice and pushing him over towards me. "After all she's in charge."

It was absolutely ridiculous, but I felt as awkward as a teenager. For goodness' sake, he was far too young for me, but I couldn't take my eyes off him. Abbie popped her head round the door.

"I'm just off out Mum...who do we have here?"

"This is..."

"Michael. Your mum's teaching me how to crochet a granny square."

Abbie just looked at me, smiled and left but I could see in her eyes what she was thinking.

"Whose idea was that?" Abbie made me a cup of tea later that night after the group had left.

"Louisa," I laughed. "I have a dreadful feeling she's trying her hand at a bit of match making."

"Bit young for you, isn't he?"

"He'll soon tire of our company, and you can keep those dirty thoughts to yourself too."

"Come on, Mum, you have to admit he's a looker. I rather like the older man myself."

"Abbie!"

"Just kidding, Mum."

I told myself I wasn't developing a crush on him but who was I kidding. I may have been on the wrong side of fifty, but I wasn't dead, well not yet anyway. What harm was there in looking.

Something kept Michael coming back week after week and I even flattered myself that it wasn't the crochet, even though he surprised us all by mastering the granny square and sharing YouTube videos on crochet techniques. He even persuaded Brian to have a go at crocheting a waistcoat of all things. Louisa couldn't believe it.

"You've got hidden talents bro. Just look at you, Mum would be proud."

"No, she wouldn't, she'd have been too drunk to notice."

"Yeah well, I'm proud of you. You'll make someone a great husband one of these days." Louisa said this rather too loudly and I lost count of how many rows of half trebles I was meant to be doing.

"Anyone fancy yarn bombing?" said Michael, giving me a particularly warm smile. I was looking at his teeth now as well as his hands. What was the matter with me?

"I'd love to," I found myself saying. "Why don't we meet up for a coffee in the week, and we can plan it out. I saw they yarn bombed Thirsk a while back, the pictures looked amazing."

"Sure, that would be great."

Morag nudged Candice.

"What's yarn bombing?" said Brian, shaping the armhole of the waistcoat like a pro.

"Decorating trees and lampposts with knitting and crochet," said Morag.

"I rather fancy decorating a telephone box," said Candice.

"That all sounds rather ambitious for a first attempt," I said, still trying to believe I'd asked Michael out. But it wasn't a date, just a coffee. "Let's yarn bomb the square, just the benches and some bollards."

"We could crochet bunting to wrap around the trees," added Morag.

"How about you, Louisa?"

"Count me out. I've been seeing a bloke called Frank and he's asked me to go away with him. Just a few days, you know, what they call a city break."

"Where are you going?" said Morag.

"Ah...Skegness," said Louisa now engrossed in her second square of crochet which was nothing like a square really.

"I'm not sure Skegness is a city," said Candice.

"You mean you're going on a dirty weekend by the sea," said Morag.

Louisa stuffed her crochet in her handbag and got up to leave.

"She's only joking, sis," said Michael.

"She's just jealous," laughed Candice.

We all laughed, and Michael caught my hand under the table and squeezed it, and I nearly died. No one had touched me in so long I'd forgotten what it felt like.

I felt like a girl going on her first date when I wriggled into my favourite dress and dug out my lipstick. But I needn't have bothered. Men are all the same, aren't they?

Michael was sitting in the cafe waiting all right, with a crisp cream shirt that made him look more delicious than usual, but he was sitting with a young woman, all red curls and lips and I'm sure she wasn't wearing a bra. Even when it was really cold my nipples never protruded that much.

"Maggie, this is Janice, my...girlfriend."

Janice looped her arm through his and pulled him closer. "Soon to be fiancé," she purred into his ear.

It was the closest I'd ever come to wanting to pour a latte over someone's head but somehow, I managed to take a seat, but words eluded me. Something in the way Michael looked at me suggested he was saying sorry in a non-verbal kind of way, but I ignored him and ordered a mug of tea.

"I'm rather jealous of your "Hooked on Crochet" group," said Janice, sprinkling sweetener into her coffee. "But Michael says I can't join. Well, I can't crochet, that's for sure."

"Yarn bombing," I said, trying to pull myself together.

"I have some designs," said Michael, swiping through

pictures on his phone.

Even though I looked at the images that streamed across the screen all I could think about was how stupid I had been, that for one second, I thought someone like Michael would even consider me.

"How did your date with Michael go, Mum?" called Abbie later that evening as I sat eating a bar of chocolate in front of the news at ten.

"It wasn't a date." Motley lay sprawled on my lap. Bracken rested her head on my knee. It was as if the cats knew comfort eating when they saw it. "It was a meeting, and he brought his soon to be fiancé along with him."

"Bastard!" said Abbie, throwing herself on the sofa and taking a chunk of chocolate. "Men just aren't to be trusted. I guess he won't be coming here again."

But Abbie was wrong, he did. That Wednesday there he was, swatches of Tunisian crochet in hand and a larger-than-life smile but thankfully, no Janice. In my dreams I'd already boiled her bunny and sent her hate mail, and it would have been rather awkward to see her sitting in my caravan. There was no Louisa either, she was out having a curry with Frank, building on the success of Skegness.

I was making the coffee when Michael appeared beside me at the tiny caravan cooker top.

"I'm sorry about the other day," he said. "I wasn't expecting Janice, she turned up out of the blue as if everything was as it was before she threw me out. You looked awkward, I'm sorry."

Awkward! I looked awkward! I was heartbroken but of course I was only deluding myself again that anyone would be interested in someone like me, rather too wide in the hips and hair that would never make a shampoo advert.

"Don't be daft," I said, spooning in the sugar. "I'm pleased she's back. Louisa told me how much she'd upset you."

Michael took the mug of coffee, brushing his hand against mine. I could feel his breath on my neck, smell his aftershave.

"Let's get cracking with the yarn bombing ladies," said Michael. "And gentlemen."

Brian gave a thumbs up. He was wearing the waistcoat he'd crocheted, and it made him look so smart. I'd taken a picture of it on my phone for Abbie to upload to our Facebook page. We had thirty new followers it seemed. Abbie was talking about starting a blog. I had no idea what a blog was.

And so, we crocheted, that night and for a month after that. Michael never mentioned Janice again and I never asked. Louisa didn't return, too busy going out with Frank it seemed. The day of the yarn bombing had arrived. Fifty individually crocheted items to be tied to the bench and bunting to wrap around the tree. I'd crocheted a bird to tie on top of one of the bollards. Brian had packed a flask of coffee and a torch and after dark we assembled in the town square. Michael was late, very late. We'd already tied crochet all over the bench by the time he arrived.

"What time do you call this?" said Morag.

"Janice keep you busy, did she?" said Candice.

I carried on stringing bunting around the tree. Michael stood behind me. He placed his hand on my shoulder. "Let me do that."

The moon shone silver in the sky. The streets were deserted but I guess not many people went out walking after midnight. I shivered. He reached into his pocket and pulled out a large, crocheted heart which he hung from one of the branches. A breeze blew my hair over my eyes. Michael pushed it away.

"She's gone and she won't be back."

"You mean, Janice? I'm sorry."

The heart spun above us.

"I'm not." And he kissed me, and he kept on kissing me until we heard Brian coughing behind us. When we turned round Morag and Candice had joined him and Abbie clicked her phone.

"A perfect picture for the new blog. I'm going to call this blog post, *Hooked on Love*."

Everyone laughed but I was too busy kissing Michael to hear them.

Dawn Treacher has three novels currently published by Provoco, The Seeds of Murder, A Deadly Plot and The Ninth Life of Norris. All can be found at Amazon and in selected retailers worldwide. Dawn's MG children's books are published by Tiny Tree Publishing.

Bottled Up

By Emma Hardy

Hope slumped down in her armchair and threw the After Eights box across the room. "Too Much" by the Spice Girls was Christmas Number One, and after listening to it on repeat, she pressed stop on her Walkman. Too much was exactly how life felt. The same way the Queen had seemed in her speech this year too, skirting around Princess Diana's death. She pulled up her blanket, took off her paper crown (another sad reminder that she'd had to pull a cracker by herself to get one) and sighed.

Christmas alone was never good, but Christmas in a Cornish holiday home was even more dire. What was she thinking coming here? But she'd been stupid enough to pay for it all, hadn't she. As usual, Max hadn't paid a penny to support one of their trips. Bastard. She shivered despite wearing four layers.

The only thing keeping her going was the Boxing Day Sea Swim that posters were advertising around the town. That was something she couldn't do if she'd stayed in London. She'd brought a swimming costume knowing the home had a hot tub, this was an additional stroke of luck. Hope peeled herself off to bed, knocking over the empty wine bottle as she got up.

The next day, Hope was up bright and early. The weather was dry, and Hope only needed three layers outside. Not bad considering it was Boxing Day.

The swim was due to start at 10.45 a.m., but at 10 a.m., the sea already looked full of people bobbing around in their Santa hats. Hope leaned closer to the window to get a better look before putting on her thick coat, scarf and hat.

It was only a short walk to the beach and Hope had already identified a cove she could safely put her belongings in as no one was there to hold them. She observed the other people entering the sea first. Some ran in, got it over with. Others dipped their toe than ran out shouting "It's freezing" to their loved ones. Hope decided to aim for a middle option - a gentle trot in to gain a bit of momentum. Water glided over her feet. She shivered but edged forward. That hit the ankle. She jogged in a bit further. The knee – oh, the knee was the worst yet. Not far to go now. She was waist deep. That was enough. The waves weren't too choppy, so she bobbed at the right time until one splashed over her neck. Goosebumps rose on top of her skin. It was in that moment that Hope couldn't decide if she was half dead or the most alive she had ever felt. Somehow, it felt empowering doing it alone. There were a few smiles across the waves until Hope decided that was enough.

Only a few steps away from where she stood, she felt something roll against her foot.

"Please don't be a jellyfish." That would be her luck. It followed her in the sand. It didn't seem to be fish of any kind, so she rolled it along until the water was shallow enough to pick it up off the sand. A glass bottle. One for the recycling, once she was redressed. That's the price paid for having a bar on the beach, a glass beer bottle enters the sea. Only on a closer inspection, it looked like an old bottle, and one that had something stuck in it. Hope rushed back to her belongings, dried herself off, and laid her spare towel out on the floor to further inspect.

Once dried off, and a towel robe draped around her, Hope saw the bottle had a rolled-up bit of paper in. Surely not? She tugged at the paper but couldn't get it out. The only way would be to smash it.

Hope headed towards the bar, which was open for warm refreshments. A tall young guy at a hot chocolate stand frowned at her as she walked past.

"Bit early for that isn't it? Bloody emmets."

"Excuse me?"

"Go home, drunken emmet."

"Firstly, my name is Hope, not Emmett and second of all,

I'm not drinking at this hour; I came across what looks like being a message in a bottle and I can't get the paper out."

"Emmet is a name we use for tourists - Latin for ant, actually. Seems like I judged you a little harshly there, Hope. Apologies. I hate it when people disrespect the sea. Can we start over? I'm Gabriel. Message in a bottle, you say. Can I look?"

"Fine. Gabriel."

"Call me Gabe."

He shook the bottle and poked his eye down it's spout to no avail.

"It'd be a shame to ruin the bottle; it looks antique in itself." He spun the green bottle in his hand.

"I guess it must have got in there somehow. So, it should come out."

Gabe walked into the bar holding the bottle without saying anything else to Hope. After what felt like an age, he returned with the paper still folded, but out of the bottle. Hope stood there, mouth open and couldn't take her eyes off the paper.

"How did you-?"

"With the help of kitchen utensils. I thought I'd leave you to read it, I haven't opened it."

"Righto. Okay. Thanks, I guess."

Hope took a deep breath as she unfolded the letter.

The paper was a crispy yellow, and the handwriting was scrawly.

June 1940, France.

My darling Joy.

I doubt this will even reach you, but no harm in trying! I have now been apart from you for four whole months and yet it feels like an eternity. I think this war will go on for a while, and all I want to do is come home to you to watch the waves at Perranporth beach with you in my arms as my wife. All this will be forgotten, and we'll be man and wife. I think about our laughs on the beach often, before all this. Our memories keep me going. We lost another young lad in our regiment last week and I promise, you'll have your lad home as soon as he can get there. Chin up. Soon Miss Anderson, you'll be Mrs Jack Latimer.

All my love, always.
Jack.

Hope folded it back into its known creases and a stray tear fell down her face.

"I wonder what happened to them both. I hope he came home." Hope looked up at Gabriel with big eyes for some reason hoping he'd have all the answers but all he could do was shake his head.

"Well. There is a Joy lives up the hill just here. I wonder if it's the same woman. But she never married."

They were interrupted with a few wet swimmers needing large hot chocolates. Hope sat back on a rock, reading and rereading the note.

"Poor Joy."

Gabe came and sat beside her. "We need to take her this note. It has to be her. She's been the town's grandmother for as long as I can remember."

"Is she okay, though? She must be in her seventies."

"Yes, she had her seventieth a few years back in the town hall. Cracking turn out. She's less mobile than she used to be, but she's of a perfectly sound mind. Give me an hour and we'll pop over to her?"

Hope nodded and headed back to the holiday home for a much-needed shower, coffee and a biscuit. The bottle and note didn't leave her sight. An hour passed, and Gabriel knocked on the door.

"How did you know I was staying here?"

"I watched you walk back, silly."

Hope took the letter and bottle and put them in her rucksack. Gabe and Hope walked in silence to Joy's cottage. If he noticed her Spice Girls badges on her bag, he was gentlemanly enough not to comment.

By the time they got to Joy's cottage, Hope could feel that she was bright red in the face and gasping for air. Gabe looked at her, grinned and rang the doorbell.

"Coming!" came an elderly voice from inside the house.

After what felt like an age, a stooped over figure with a walking stick opened the door.

"Gabriel, dear. Why… is everything okay? Your dad…?"

"Everything's fine, Joy, don't worry. This is Hope - she's staying at Rodney's gaff."

"Oh, Miss Moneybags. Surprised you've picked up an emmet, Gabriel, thought I taught you better than that."

"No, well, yes, but I think she's found something on the beach that belongs to you."

Gabriel held up the bottle.

Joy frowned. "You'd better both come in."

Hope and Gabe looked at each other before entering Joy's property.

"I'm not as good on my feet as I used to be, so I have some biscuits out, but Gabe if you want a cuppa, you know where everything is."

"We're good, thanks, Joy. Don't worry about hospitality."

"I'm a Cornishwoman, it's what we do."

The house smelt of 'Nice' biscuits. There was a silence which was too long to break, Hope couldn't believe that she'd found herself in a sitting room with an old lady and a surfer guy on Boxing Day. She looked over at Gabe. He had to kick this off.

"Joy. I think Hope has found something on the beach that belongs to you."

He handed over the note. "It was found in this." He passed her the bottle.

Hope again found herself in a silence, but watched Joy's face drop as she got to the end. Then Joy folded it neatly back up and handed it back to Gabe who looked confused.

"Joy?"

"I don't know where to start." She stood up and went to her dresser. Turning back around, she had a shoebox in her hand. Gabe jumped up to take it off her so she could safely sit back down in her armchair.

"I got this letter from the army in May 1940 saying he was missing, presumed dead, but this is dated June 1940. I never heard from him again after the army note. Until now."

Hope reached for the shoebox. "Do you mind if I?"

"Go ahead, dear." Joy didn't look at Hope.

As Joy said, the army letter was dated a month prior.

"What was he thinking a message in a bottle? It's his handwriting, I know that much. And if he survived, where did he go? Because he didn't come here."

The next item in the shoebox was a black and white photo of them on the beach, smiling and embracing. It must have been pre-war.

"What do we do now?" Gabe looked over at Hope.

"Well, we need to find him, if we can. Joy, tell us everything you know."

Hours went by and Hope felt like a detective, trying to pull very few clues together. Joy talked endlessly about their backstory, meeting on the beach and having a seaweed fight. But nothing since the letter saying he was missing. Until the message in a bottle.

Out of nowhere, Gabe stood up. "We must go to the West Briton with this and see if the paper can find him."

"But he wasn't Cornish, dear, I'm ashamed to admit he was from Devon."

"Fraternising with the enemy, Joy, and you had the cheek to say I arrived with an emmet today!"

Joy blushed.

"Sorry, Hope. I was just so shocked to see Gabe with a woman, well. Since… you know." Joy coughed and stopped talking. Hope glanced over at him, but he couldn't seem to look in her direction.

He changed the conversation. "First thing tomorrow, we're going to the newspaper office. Joy, how would it feel to be front page of the local rag?"

"Oh, I'm pleased I've had my perm done this week. I'm ready!"

"Hope - I'll pick you up in my Ford Escort tomorrow, okay? It's a burgundy one."

Hope nodded. What a day. And what would tomorrow bring?

As promised, at 10 a.m. on the dot, Gabe rocked up outside

where Hope was staying. Hope clutched the newly found treasure. She even slept with it on the bedside table last night out of sheer paranoia. But she wouldn't admit that to anyone else. Radio One blasted through the car. But after the Teletubbies song followed by Aqua's Barbie Girl, Gabe hit the power button on his cassette player. It was seconds later before they parked up in front of the West Briton offices which had the blinds closed. Gabe jumped out but the offices were locked shut.

"Holiday season is over now, surely its back to news?"

"Wait, what day is it?"

"The twenty-seventh!"

"No, not date, day."

"Saturday. It's Saturday isn't it."

Hope sighed. "Yes."

It was a long drive back in silence before Gabe popped in to tell Joy they'd got a bit carried away. He reported back to Hope that she'd laughed and said they were just like her getting their days mixed up.

"What now?" Gabe asked.

"I don't know."

"Want a free surfing lesson?"

"You can surf?"

"I'm a certified instructor, and Cornish, so, yeah. Let's do it. I have a spare women's wet suit in the house; it looks about your size. Just don't ask where it came from."

"Deal."

Within minutes of leaving Gabe's cottage, Hope was crouched on a surfboard trembling.

"You can do this, Hope."

"I can't."

They hadn't even gone very deep. Hope fell off a few times and, in the end, marched out the water, admitting defeat.

Gabe walked her back to her house, and she could tell he was stifling laughter. She'd felt so stupid for even trying to surf. Hope went inside her holiday home and was sure she could hear him burst out laughing as she shut her door. But when she peered out the window, Gabe had gone. Maybe she was a city girl after all.

Monday arrived and as before they drove to the West Briton offices which were open. Gabe knew the Head of News and straight away, he ushered them into a side room with a Dictaphone in hand. They retold Joy's story to Tim who listened intently and didn't seem to be giving them lip service.

"Guys, this is front page news - and Joy's all right with having her photo taken?"

"Oh, yes, she told us her perm is ready." Gabe smirked.

"Have you gone to anyone else about this? Pirate FM? Radio Cornwall?"

"Oh, we hadn't thought of that. No."

"Great. We have the exclusive. Tell Joy a photographer will be with her at 2 p.m., and she'll be front page in Thursday's edition. We'll make this a national sensation, and more importantly, find Jack."

Hope jolted. Would Jack still be alive? Would he have his memory? What was his story? They have a fifty-seven-year gap to fill. It was starting to feel very real.

"Hope- are you okay? You've gone white."

"Yes, thanks, just a lot to take in, isn't it?"

"Are you thinking of your surfing attempt on Saturday?" Gabe gave her a playful nudge.

"No. I AM NOT." It would be a long day.

On the dot at 2 p.m. Hope answered the door to Snappy. She didn't know his real name as he introduced himself on the doorstep as his nickname.

"Snappy's here," she shouted to Joy and Gabe.

"Ah, Darren, nice to see you." Gabe shook his hand.

Darren then. Of course, Gabe knew him. It was clear that everyone knew everyone round here.

"Now Joy, how do you feel about a photo shoot on the beach? Are you up to it? I'll drive us down."

"Ooh, I'll say, let me get my sun hat."

"It's December, Joy. You won't need that."

"Just for old times' sake," she called back.

It appeared very quickly that Joy was a natural in front of a camera. This also was a surprise to no-one. She held the bottle up jokily, then read the letter with a tear in her eye.

"I used to be in all the local am drams, you know."

"She once played all three witches in Macbeth." Gabe whispered in Hope's ear.

"I once played all three witches in Macbeth. They couldn't find anyone with a good enough witch voice." Joy held the bottle like a magic wand.

Hope nearly tripped up in the sand, she was laughing so hard and Gabe caught her.

Snappy piped up. "That was just like the photo of Joy and Jack. Let's reenact that for the paper too. Gabe stand here."

"No, I don't think we should do that," Hope said.

Gabe ignored her and pulled her into position standing in front of him as he put his arms around her.

"Perfect couple. About time you moved on Gabe."

"Shut it, Darren."

The photoshoot was over and now came the three day wait for the West Briton.

Thursday at 8 a.m., Hope heard knocking on the door so loud she was about to scream at the person who had broken her peace. Until she realised it was Gabriel with the front page.

"Message in a bottle found 57 years on."

Joy, as expected, dazzled the front page. They both marched up the hill to Joy's who was already cutting out the front page to frame and place above her mantelpiece.

"Where did you get that from?"

"The newsagents, silly."

"How did you get there?"

"Oh, Snappy posted it through my letterbox this morning. The phone hasn't rung yet."

"Well don't get your hopes up, Joy."

"Jack will ring. I know he will."

By the sixth cup of tea of the day, Hope was flagging. She'd never drank so much tea. The landline rang all day, but it was national press wanting more quotes and information on Joy's story. No Jack. Joy had clearly loved all the attention; Hope was convinced she looked ten years younger than she had this morning. If Hope was not mistaken, the lipstick throughout the day was getting redder every hour, too.

No-one could have anticipated what the next day was going to bring. Hope and Gabriel arrived at Joy's to see at least fifty news reporters, camera crew and photographers. Joy's curtains were tightly shut.

Gabe took Hope's hand and dragged her through the front garden. Shouts from the paps could be heard but Hope put her head down and didn't say a word.

Joy was pacing the living room, shaking.

"What have I done? I only did this to find Jack and I've brought strangers to my front door. One even said he'd come all the way from London."

"Sit down, Joy. Hope, pop the kettle on. This will find Jack I'm sure of it."

"I regret it all, Gabriel, I really do."

Joy sat with her head in her hands, the national papers scattered all over the living room floor. Hope rested on the edge of the kitchen doorframe whilst the kettle boiled.

There was a knock on the door. "I can't answer it." Joy grabbed a handkerchief and dabbed her eyes.

"I'll go." Gabe opened the door. "Now listen here, inside is a vulnerable old lady, just looking for a lost love that she thought dead for nearly sixty years and now had a small ray of hope he might not be. Please leave her alone."

"You need to hear me out. I'm Jack's brother, Bernard."

Joy screamed from the living room. "Bernard! It's really you? But that means Jack hasn't come. He must be - have passed…"

"Jack is alive."

"You'd better come inside." Gabe ushered him in against the listening crowd outside.

Joy gave Bernard a hug. "I expect you don't remember me, we only met once, briefly."

"Of course I do. You are the love of Jack's life."

"Pardon?"

"You heard me, you aren't that deaf or daft, judging by all this press coverage."

"Well, I did play all three witches in Macbeth."

Hope placed a tray of four cups on the coffee table.

"Jack is on the beach. But he saw all the press and panicked. But he's here."

"Why didn't he come back to me after the war, Bernard?"

"It's a long story, that's his to tell."

Bernard and Joy spoke for hours. Hope repeatedly glanced over at Gabe but he looked so immersed in the conversation, she couldn't find a cue to leave. However, leaving could have also meant missing the big reunion whenever it was about to happen and so she was convinced that was why Gabe wouldn't look in her direction.

At 5 p.m. on the dot, the doorbell rang. Gabe instantly looked at Hope.

"I'll get it." Joy was quick to react.

Bernard, Gabe and Hope couldn't help but follow her to the door, but they crept into the downstairs toilet to they could peek at the action without intruding on the couple's re-meet.

Joy opened the door.

"My dearest Joy, can you ever forgive me?"

Hope wiped her hand over her eyes. This wasn't about her.

"Jack, I'm absolutely furious with you! How dare you keep me waiting all these years! To find out that you were alive. I hate you!" Joy slammed the door shut.

Bernard, Hope and Gabe twisted and turned around each other in the doorway of the bathroom. What on earth had just happened? What was Joy playing at? In the second they took to react and process the news; Joy had already reopened the door to see Jack holding a small box out towards her.

"My knees aren't what they used to be, so I can't get on the floor. My darling Joy, will you marry me?"

"I thought you'd never ask! Yes, of course!"

The three spectators went to the front door and clapped.

Hope shook Jack's hand. What a whirlwind. This would never have happened if she hadn't rolled her foot on a glass bottle.

"Now tell me where you've been all these years? Hope, can you make another cuppa?" Joy sat back in her armchair with a huge grin on her face.

"Never mind cuppas, I'll just pop to the bar and get a bottle of our champagne. Hope, do you want to come with?"

Hope didn't, but she knew giving them some privacy would do the newly engaged couple good. As she put her coat on, the story started unravelling.

"I came back for you after the war, but you weren't in, and the old postman told me you'd moved house, but he didn't know where."

"But I'd never moved! Was that the tall one? Moustache a bit too like Hitler?"

"That's the one."

"I turned him down, so he must have got his own back. Why, if he wasn't already dead, I'd wring his neck."

Hope raised her eyebrows at Gabe.

"Back in ten."

There came no reply.

"Well, we couldn't have wished for a better outcome could we, Hope?"

"I know. My heart sank when she slammed the door in his face. Poor Jack."

"She always had a dark sense of humour."

The couple walked in silence to the bar, and Hope felt sorry she only had a few more days in this lovely Cornish town.

"You're thinking about leaving here, aren't you." Gabe interrupted her thoughts.

"How did you know?"

"I see it on every emmet's face when they have a day or two left."

"I thought you were over calling me that."

"Sorry, yes. It was also on my ex-fiancée's."

"Oh."

"Yes. Left for London for some job in banking."

"I'm sorry."

Hope didn't know how she could leave Perranporth after everything the last week had brought her. She wrapped her coat around her tighter. The wind on the beach picked up as they turned the corner.

"Bottle of bubbly, please, pal. Can we have five glasses to take away. You know I'll bring them back." Gabe rubbed his hands together.

"There you go. And remember, I know where you live." The barman winked at the pair.

Hope carried the glasses in what looked like a wine box with a cardboard handle. Gabe marched on with a huge bottle in his hand.

"Bottle for a bottle." Hope laughed at herself.

"It's no longer bottled up." Gabe replied.

"Let's hope neither of the couple bottle it on their wedding day."

"You'll come back here for the wedding, won't you?"

The couple had reached Joy's doorstep and saw her mistletoe.

"I don't remember seeing that before." Gabe pointed.

"Me neither."

"Well, I'm not one to break tradition, are you?"

"Never."

They pair kissed as Joy opened the door and giggled.

"I knew it!"

Hope could feel her cheeks going red and decided it must have been the walk.

The West Briton were all too happy to publish the reunited couple's new story and Joy graced the front page once again with a wedding ring. The paper was so impressed with Hope's research skills they offered her a newspaper job on the spot, and she gratefully accepted.

Hope was able to rent out where she was staying for a few more months, but then the dreaded letter arrived saying that she'd need to move out. All afternoon she cried on Gabe's shoulder that she didn't want to leave the cottage, or the town and didn't know what to do.

The following morning, a green glass bottle was placed in the centre of her dining table. The sender had been thoughtful enough to make it as easy as possible to enable the paper to slide out. It had a message inside.

"Dear Hope, let's not waste another minute. Move in with me? G xx."

Hope ran out of the cottage and down the road to the bar. She saw Gabe drying the glasses. Rather than reacting, she grabbed the remote of the corner television, turned it on and watched the Big Breakfast. She stayed with her back to him and was smiling the entire time. She leant her arm back for a snack. The peanuts on the edge of the bar had soon disappeared.

"Ahem." Gabe crept up behind her and hugged her.

"Hey."

"Hello."

She spun round on her stool to face him. "Yes."

"Yes?"

"Definitely!"

Hope and Gabe kissed. Joy and Jack entered the bar.

"She said yes!"

"You can always trust a message in a bottle to capture a woman's heart."

The four-some laughed as they drank the delicious hot chocolate on Perranporth beach, ready to start their new lives together.

Emma Hardy is a debut novelist. Her first novel is due to be published by Provoco in early 2026.

Crematorium Chimney Sweep

By Nicholas Vaughan

"I am the crematorium chimney sweep, and my name is Marley. I'm employed to sweep the chimney on a day-to-day basis, for which I get paid a measly sum. The more deaths on our street the busier the crematorium is. And the more times the chimney cord is pulled by vicar Blake who works down in the church, if I don't scrub those walls clean, the chimney will block up, and the whole street will be covered in corpse ashes. And that would never do. Even though I don't like this job, I can do it with my eyes closed."

There was a hideous din, and a fresh wave of microscopic organs and the acrid smell of burnt hair came filtering through. Marley retched, then pulled up his ever-present mask around his nostrils and mouth. *At least that should keep the fumes out*, he thought.

Marley could hear the echo of Blake's voice resounding in the base of the chimney and circulating up towards him. He could make out the last prayers being read out. Then Marley was hit by black and noxious clouds, his eyes began to sting like crazy, and he burst into tears.

Marley could hear a metallic scraping as if a grating was pulled far below. Something heavy being hoisted across that would allow access from the furnace. Slowly but surely, another familiar waft pumped through. The dust rose to its highest point, then it began to fall back down like snowfall, upon every surface of the chimney, bricks, mortar and cement.

"That'll take me hours to clean," Marley said, with a grimace.

A minute later, he noticed a densely packed layer of ash and dust as it began to take on the form of a human being. Soon it became more recognizable. Then a blurry figure presented itself and said, "My name is Kent, before I passed away, I used to be a senior manager at Ford."

Marley looked up at Kent with a gone-out expression.

"You look exactly like my dad," he said.

Kent replied, "I am. Today was my final day on earth, believe me."

Marley swallowed hard, then struggling to speak, said, "It's been awful to see your demise so quickly through cancer."

"Tell me about it," replied Kent. "Imagine being the one with the malignant presence."

"And tell me, where are you heading for now?"

"I wanted to find myself in a brighter place. I was hoping for a new start," Kent told him.

Marley came and looked deep into Kent's eyes. "You look like you've seen a lot in this life."

"I've seen a lot, you're right," replied Kent. "I've also partied hard and led an unhealthy lifestyle. Wasted a lot of my life, my time."

"But you had plenty of loving family."

"Yeah, I did and I'm grateful for my sons, my grandchildren, as well as friends scattered to every corner of the earth."

"To be loved is an incredible thing. But would you have requested anymore out of life, from your time on earth?"

"I'd have loved to see my grandchildren grow up. And to attend all those life events, weddings, christenings, baptisms …even funerals."

"Look, I have one last subject I want to discuss before you leave. I must try and understand grief for myself, for the day when my numbers up."

"Okay, maybe there is more that I can tell you. Those last few days, especially with an illness, are the worst. You'll have all your loved ones screaming and beating their chests with anguish, as they can't understand why such a thing should happen."

"We didn't."

Kent ignored him and went on, "No, no, of course you

didn't. It wasn't happening to you. And the pain is endless. Anyway, enough of my death. What about your life? This is a bit of a dead-end job, isn't it? When are you going to do something with your life or are you going to be like me and regret the stuff you didn't do?"

"I haven't passed away yet, I'm still full of life. But part of me has died, well, two parts now. That's why I'm ready to get a new role and move on. It feels like an eternity since I started this job, though I know it isn't that long."

"You're exaggerating," said Kent and gave him a sidelong glance. "When I leave what will you do?"

Marley replied, "I have a vague idea. Keep on sweeping chimneys but also try to find another career. And I'll be a hell of lot more positive in the future."

"Goodbye then, son. Just keep smiling."

Then there was another piping hot gust from below, and the chimney was full of fiery particles. Marley braced his legs and readied himself for the next onslaught of darkened toxic clouds to envelope him. The scaffolding that he was stood on shook with an infernal tremor.

Suddenly the whole space was lost in clouds of dust, as if part of the chimney had fallen in. As the air began to clear, Marley coughed and spluttered. Another abstract form began to appear from the dust and choking black smog, and it gave a hacking cough.

"I'm an architect, and my name is Marlow."

"Nice to meet you," replied Marley.

"I really love my job, being an architect is the best thing ever. And it means I get to keep those creative juices flowing."

Marley said, "I hate my job, to be fair. I wish I was as artistic as you are."

"You can be, you must have an artistic bone in your body somewhere."

"Actually, you're right, I wanted to be an artist, but I didn't have any faith in myself at all. I'm still a great disbeliever in my own abilities."

Marlow looked at him for a while as if he couldn't believe

what he was hearing, then he went on.

"Go on then, pull out your chimney sweep brushes and do me a portrait."

"That's ridiculous," replied Marley. "I wouldn't even know where to start."

"I can see where the lack of confidence comes in!"

"It's always been that way, that's why I ended up taking work in another area."

"I'm not hearing it," he cried out. "Get those brushes out and do your best likeness of me."

"Perhaps, I could have a go. Just for old times' sake."

Marlow pushed him bodily into one corner of the scaffolding.

"You've got a charming angle to paint from."

Marley found a place to sit and pulled out his brushes.

"This sure beats scrubbing ash and bodily fluids from the walls," Marley said.

He pulled out one of his finest brushes, then began to busy himself with measuring up.

"I'm limbering up," said Marley, "it's been a while since I've done this."

Marlow went on, "Okay, I'll have patience."

There was quiet between them for what seemed like an age.

Finally, he cried out, "I've no patience to be a sitter."

Marlow, ever eager to see how his portrait was coming along, jumped up to go and see.

He stared over Marley's shoulder for a while, "You're amazing," he said. "You've got a perfect likeness of me. Why do you have so little faith in yourself?"

"I'm not sure," and Marley stared at the floor timidly, as if trying to avoid Marlow's scrutiny.

"You're an unbelievable artist. One in a million, why can't you see that?"

"I really struggle with being able to take criticism."

Marlow replied, "I can't understand that, as I've always been able to take feedback onboard, then use it to improve my practise. Perhaps you need to change your way of thinking, otherwise the world will suffer greatly from your loss."

"That's amazing to hear, because it means you're telling me the truth, and not just talking out of your rear end, which I know a lot of people do these days."

"Believe me, my brother," went on Marlow, "and more importantly, believe in yourself, but only if you can make it out of that mundane day-to-day existence of chimney sweeping."

With that there was silence, and Marley was left scratching away again. He took one last long look at the portrait and then smiled with satisfaction to himself. Unfortunately, there was nobody else to see his artistry. Then he saw another cloud of smoke and ash billowing up the chimney.

There was a rush of baking hot air which turned the inner part of the chimney into a kiln. Marley stepped backwards and then leapt forwards again after he singed his trouser leg on the wall. He steadied himself, then took a better grip on his brush. *I best be getting on,* he thought.

Abruptly, a great dark shadow descended upon the interior of the chimney, then a figure burst forth. Marley ducked to the floor, gripping his hands over his head. Then a voice erupted from the midst of the hovering, grainy mass.

"I'm Quintin," it announced. "And you can all take a seat and bow down to me. Why is life so different for a clever chap like me. An inventor. Every project I begin becomes second nature to me. Every book I open easy to understand. Everything I touch turns to gold."

That really wound Marley up, and he began hopping from one foot to the other.

"You are a rotten toerag," he cried out. "Why do some people find it so easy to make a living at anything they try!"

Quintin was on fire, now he realised he had got poor Marley on the run.

"I know your type," he said, in an overconfident voice. "Always struggling to find work, always chopping and changing career."

"I've heard enough about how intelligent you are, and how every little thing falls with ease into your lap."

Quintin went on gassing away. "Yes, and then on day three I

started a third job, but I didn't really have to, as I'm so overqualified. Then I have time to breathe easy, think about life, before rushing into decisions about this and that. And not to mention the constant holidays. They're back-to-back for me."

Marley cursed Quintin beneath his breath.

"Why is life such a breeze for some people," he said. "Why can't the tables be switched for once?"

Quintin replied, "That's not the way things are supposed to be."

Marley ran at the fellow, even though he had perched himself up on a brick wall and was lecturing away. Quintin kept up his tirade, blissfully unaware of the poor chap at his feet who was tearing his hair out. Then he noticed him.

"Oi, you, sling your bleeding hook," he shouted, "you heard me, get out of here. Unless you can pay me in a way that's reasonable?"

Marley narrowed his eyes, and replied, "I can paint well enough, but I'd rather not waste the effort."

There was an awkward silence and, fuming with rage, Marley climbed back up on to his scaffolding.

Quintin went on discussing his life, and his business engagements for the next week or so. Then he ran out of things to say, leaped down from the wall, and began to shake the tower Marley was stood on.

"With a bit of luck, I can knock the bugger flying."

"Oi, less of that, I don't want to be seasick."

There was no reply from Quintin who went on in his usual besotted self-delusional way.

As he was lost in his own selfish outburst, Marley muttered in a low voice, "Why don't I paint his portrait anyway, sometimes the best subjects are the ones who are the maddest."

And with that he pulled up a spare brush that happened to be nearby, and began using its tip to scratch away, to try and measure how overinflated his ego was.

Quintin began accusing the rest of the world for its own

ineffectiveness, and yelled out, "And not to mention the meek and lowly!"

That was a sensitive spot for Marley who had had enough of biting and accurate remarks.

"All my life, I've had to deal with comments from people, cutting me down low."

Quintin ran and shoved the scaffolding that Marley was sat atop. It quaked, and he took a tumble to the floor.

"You're banned from my chimney," cried out Marley, as he jumped up. "I shouldn't have to put up with aggressive bullies that talk to me as if I can't understand."

There was a grating sound down below, as vicar Blake threw another body to the flames.

"It must be another cremation," muttered Marley. "Thank God for that, my luck's in!"

He ran to one side and took cover. He had the feeling that another presence might make itself known. When he looked again, Marley could see another figure had taken Quintin's place, and was sat on top of his scaffolding, manicuring his nails and preening himself. The individual stood up and announced himself.

"I am the world-famous actor, Auden. You could be the next big thing, too. Never mind hiding behind an easel the whole day painting, or cleaning in a cupboard."

"As it goes, I quite enjoy that existence. Why can't you understand that not everybody wants to be the same."

"I disagree completely. You should go against the grain."

"That's not for me. I like my own company and making observations in a visual way."

"Why don't you try and change though?"

"Not a chance, that's not for me. I prefer to be my own person; from there I can look out at the world and see it in a more individual way."

"I can understand you don't want to change, but nevertheless I'm going to keep up my relentless argument to the counter."

Marley replied, "This guy's not even listening to me either … What a day."

"If I were to change my line of banter. Instead of asking you to change a lot, it would be just a tiny bit, occasionally. And you could aim for something far closer to how you are already."

"That perhaps I could swallow, if it's not such a great turnaround in my personality. I could really benefit with the boost in confidence. Mine is in tatters after so many years of self-hatred and not believing I had any talents."

"Okay, so we might be onto something here. So, you are agreeing to change, that's a delight to hear! You haven't been the easiest man to win over though, to be fair."

"Why would I? I just told you what an awful time I've had growing up, constantly beating myself up over every little thing."

"The first thing that you need to do is brush up your appearance," Auden said, "a new suit wouldn't go amiss either."

"That's not my fault really, as I work all week. Of course, my clothes would be drab and dirty."

Auden stared into the distance as if he hadn't heard.

After a while, Marley said, "Okay, that could be doable. But I guess this would have to happen after I get back out from the chimney."

"Of course," replied Auden. "You need to take on a new persona to draw back that curtain."

"I'll see what I can do when I finally get out of here."

Auden said, "I believe in you."

"The old me must go, and then my self-worth will grow."

"I love the sound of that," he said. "I'm beginning to get an idea of the real Marley. Now I've come to an agreement with you, I need to leave."

"Just wait for a moment, I need to make some form of payment."

"No, really, just having had a tiny impact on your life is enough."

"My characters changed so much; you've had such a positive

outlook of me. Let me take up my brushes and offer to capture your generous profile."

"I'd be honoured."

"Stand up against the chimney breast, and I'll sketch out your outline. Then I can work into once you're gone."

"I would much rather take it with me now."

"Yeah, of course. I'll dash off a quick likeness. But it'll be more like a caricature though."

"That'll be fine, so long as you don't exaggerate any of my facial features."

"Why would I do that? You've taught me to how to adapt."

Marley's brow was furrowed, as he frantically sketched away. After some time, he put his brush to one side.

Auden stepped over and took one long glance at the work. "I'm totally enamoured," he cried out. "I love it! But how can I take it with me?"

Marley had sketched it into the grime on the walls, and there wasn't a chance it would budge.

"It will have to be from memory then," Auden said.

"Sometimes that's the best way," replied Marley.

Auden stared long and hard at his portrait, memorizing every detail.

Marley said, "It's been emotional."

"Let me say thanks with a big hug," Auden replied, in a choked voice. "It's difficult for me to be so open about myself sometimes."

"So, you also need to change, if you're not one hundred percent perfect."

"I thought I was."

Marley hugged Auden, and said, "I can't even speak, I'm about to burst out crying. This is as bad as when my dad died earlier on today."

Then he began sobbing uncontrollably. Auden let his little body shake, until it had released all its pent-up emotion.

"You should never hold it in, it's not good for your soul," he said to a shiny eyed Marley.

After a while, the tears dried on his cheek, then Marley stuttered out. "I can't thank you enough for all of this, you're like an old friend that never wants to leave. But I know you must go."

A gust of wind swept through the chimney and blew the painting from the wall.

Auden with surprise, exclaimed, "What a calamity, the artwork disappeared. I never figured it would happen that quickly."

Marley replied, "You're not wrong there. And after all that effort to change myself."

"You did though, in so many ways."

"I did what I could. At least you committed it to memory."

Nicholas Vaughan's debut novel for Provoco, The Unwrapping, was published in October 2025 and is available from Amazon and selected retailers worldwide.

The Assassin's Rule (or The Assassin's Christmas Gift)

By A H Martin

There is one rule that I've never intentionally broken ever since I involuntarily parted company with my British government handlers. Don't ever ask me to target a child or teenager, nor put me in a position that could force me to harm one. My agency contact arrogantly insisted that the target's family, including three children, were legitimate collateral damage, and for that arrogance, he paid the ultimate price. The agency high-ups were less than happy with my solution, and after I went rogue, I've been on their 'Remove with prejudice' list.

Usually, I undertake contracts I believed were morally acceptable. My area of expertise was the ability to make an assassination seem accidental, although I wasn't adverse to employ poison, a bullet, knife or garrote. I will work for the so-called bad guys; remember, one man's bad guy is another's hero.

So, I'm freezing my arse off in a borrowed Elf costume better suited for a porn shoot in a Santa grotto in the middle of a winter wonderland. The previous owner of the said costume had gleefully accepted my offer of the paid vacation in Spain. It hasn't taken me long to understand why she'd been so keen to accept my offer as I kept fending off Santa's attempts to grope said freezing part of my anatomy.

I'd give him one more opportunity to consider the folly of his actions. Then I was going to break one of the fat slob's offending digits. Given the copious amount of vodka he had added to his coffee flask, I doubt he would feel it. The thick red cape would hide the evidence and allow him to keep working.

So why was one of the world's premier assassins freezing her arse off in a poorly heated log cabin in Lapland, considering digital homicide? When I could be drinking vodka wrapped in furs at the nearby Ice hotel, enjoying the company of the attractive receptionist.

Good question!

I flinched, damn it! I'd warned him. The sound of the joint snapping and the associated anguished scream were music to my ears.

I'm here because of the fallout from a contract I'd accepted several weeks earlier. The details forwarded from the Broker had been inviting and, in hindsight, too easy. The target had a long history of involvement with organised crime, drugs, protection, and human trafficking. The latter was the clinching argument; I despise human traffickers. Just the type of contract I was known to take, and the fee wasn't to be sniffed at either. Someone was willing to pay big bucks to get him out of the way.

I acknowledged interest, and the Broker forwarded the target's background file; like most files from this Broker, the target's name was withheld. In some ways, I preferred not to know; it made what I did less personal.

The file outlined that the target's family had been longstanding members of the local criminal Brotherhood. He had become the head after the untimely death of his older brother. There was no other immediate family still alive; both parents also died under suspicious circumstances when he was a teenager. The target's home was a secure mountain chalet on the south side of a steep-sided valley, several hundred metres above the valley floor.

A private narrow road guarded by a security checkpoint and guardhouse led up the valley side to the chalet on a rise at the head of the valley. Each morning, an SUV collected him, and drove him to his office, returning in the evening.

The photos showed a dark, brooding rock above the chalet, thickly covered in snow at this time of the year. The overhang gave the impression that it had been there for eternity. Solid and stable, providing the chalet protection from avalanches.

The contract ticked all my boxes as; after perusing the documentation, I could see how to fulfil it without getting my hands dirty. My initial impression suggested the overhang had a weakness. Three carefully placed explosive charges detonated in sequence, and the whole lot would rapidly sweep down the valley side in a massive avalanche and obliterate the chalet and anybody inside. It would be so rapid that it wouldn't give the target any opportunity to react. Best of all, if I did my job correctly, it would look like a natural disaster.

During the day and into the early evening, a housekeeper and a chef were present, and as far as I could see, both were unaware of the target's criminal dealings. After confirming they had left, I would blow the charges. They had families, and as such were not acceptable collateral.

Following several days of preparation and reconnaissance, I had hiked into position using the cover of the late afternoon shadows, staying below the valley's rim. The snow didn't deter me; I was in my work mode, focused and prepared. My backpack was weighed down with the three remotely triggered explosive charges I'd need, plus a spare. My favourite armourer made them after I had described my intention, each consisting of a kilo and a half of Semtex and a remote detonator in a light alloy container.

The pack also held the remote detonator transmitter, powerful lowlight binoculars, ammunition for my heavily customised Accuracy International Arctic Warfare rifle, a light tent, and enough provisions to sustain me for two days. It was a fair weight, but one I was accustomed to.

On the first evening, I watched from the lookout point I'd chosen as the target's vehicle returned to the security of his chalet. Through the powerful binoculars, I could easily confirm the presence of the target accompanied by a driver who doubled as a bodyguard. After a few minutes, the SUV and the driver left and stopped at the guardhouse. The housekeeper left an hour later and the chef soon after.

I'd anticipated setting off the explosives tomorrow evening after placing them during the day. I would only press the trigger after confirming the target was alone. That would have given me the rest of the night to fade away. The timing would hinder rescue attempts in the improbable scenario that the target survived the avalanche.

That morning, snow had begun to fall as I planted the charges. Three charges were evenly spaced along a fissure running across the base of the outcrop. After a few moments of consideration, I had decided to place the spare fourth charge in the snow that had built up along the top of the ridge. According to my calculations, about a two-hundred-meter-wide section of the valley side, consisting of large rocks, trees, and snow, would sweep down, obliterating the chalet and a fair portion of the access road. It might even reach the main road.

After placing the explosives and removing any evidence of my actions. I had retreated to my chosen lookout point, giving me an uninterrupted view of the track up to the chalet, and a distant view of the main road.

The cold was beginning to seep through my insulated camouflage suit before the lights of the returning SUV appeared at the gatehouse. There had been an earlier false alarm three-quarters of hour ago as a couple of vehicles had driven up. One had left after a few minutes, and the second, a green van, hadn't returned. It seemed like a routine delivery, and should leave soon, but in my line of business, nothing was routine.

I had managed to survive for as long as possible by listening to my instincts, which were buzzing now. Something about the timing of the van's arrival felt wrong. The previous day, I noted delivery vans arriving, but they left after a few minutes. None had stayed as long as the green van currently parked by the side of the chalet.

Initially I'd ignored the van, now I studied it intensively. Peering through the binoculars, I'd finally made out a logo and writing and felt my heart lurch. Emblazoned on the side was a pair of cartoon clowns, and the words, 'Children's Party Entertainers,' in the local language. The what? Shit, what the actual hell! Why was a children's entertainer at the chalet?

The SUV pulled up at the entrance to the chalet, and a woman and two young children appeared in the lit doorway. Where the hell had they come from? There was not supposed to be anyone in the place other than the chef and housekeeper, both of whom should be leaving.

The children hurried to the target's side, and he gathered them in his arms. The woman warmly greeted him with a hug and a kiss. A family. One that was not on my agenda! Shit!

I needed to know more, as nothing felt right. The information I'd received from the Broker was supposed to have been an intense deep dive. It had stated several times that the target was unmarried and lived alone. What I had seen was directly counter to the information I'd been given. And if that was incorrect, what else was?

Several more expensive-looking vehicles passed through the checkpoint, heading towards the chalet. Each disgorged several children and adults, greeted by the target and his wife. Most of the parents carried colourfully wrapped presents. I carefully removed the battery from the transmitter; I wanted no accidental explosions that evening. This hit was busted.

I could feel my anger growing; this was turning into a cluster fuck. How the hell had this happened? Everyone I worked with knew about my rule.

I'd called the Broker on my Sat phone only to be shunted to an answering service, informing me that the Broker was unavailable. This was never supposed to happen while the contract was active.

Then I had called the only person I believed would give me a straight answer. Simone was an independent information broker and occasional lover; of course, I had her unlisted number. I'd worked with Simone, and her information had always been accurate.

A voice with a French accent answered the call and asked cautiously. "Who is this?"

"Simone, it's Verity. I've got a situation and need your skills," I replied.

"If it is you, then you should be able to tell me the last time we met," she asked sarcastically.

I smiled to myself, knowing that Simone had recognised my voice. I guessed she was pissed at me as I hadn't been in touch for several months. "It was that beautiful weekend at the St. Regis in Rome, which we need to do again." Then I repeated, "I really need your help."

She replied in a much more relaxed tone, "For you, ma cherie, of course."

I outlined the situation I found myself in. "I need to know all about the target and who would want him dead," I concluded.

"And you weren't given the target's name?"

"No," I admitted. "That's usually irrelevant in this type of contract. The only personal details I was given were his location and that his family are connected to the Croatian criminal Brotherhood."

"A dangerous group. Let me know the location, and I'll see what I can find. This is going to cost you. Call me back in three hours and I will let you know what I've turned up.2

She ended the call before I could say anything else, and I continued to watch the chalet. Behind the tall windows, I caught glimpses of the children playing games, and my anger grew by the minute. I wouldn't be leaving until I'd made the charges safe and disposed of them. And that was a job for a rested mind in the morning.

The cold seeped into my bones, even with the Arctic survival training I had undergone. I found a concealed hollow near my overwatch hide and erected the shelter. Which meant I could risk a small fire without being spotted and have a warm meal. At the appointed time, I called Simone.

"What the fuck have you got yourself involved with?" were

the first words out of her mouth. The anxiety in her voice was all the confirmation I needed. She continued. "Almost everything you said was in the info pack was a fictitious legend. Your target's name is Marko Novac, and I can find nothing that ties him to the Brotherhood. There's a sister, and two brothers; one of whom is dead. The dead brother was the only link to the Brotherhood I could uncover. He was on the periphery of one of the Brotherhood's lesser operations. But he died in a traffic accident five years ago."

"Definitely an accident?"

"Oui, a simple case of wrong place, wrong time. Because of his association with the Brotherhood, it was thoroughly investigated, and an unfortunate accident was ruled. Marko is married and has two children, twins, a boy, and a girl, who are five years old. He's the CEO of a successful international engineering conglomerate based in Rijeka. They've got contracts all over the world."

The sickening feeling I'd been played wrenched at me. "Are you sure there's nothing that links him to the Brotherhood?"

"Nothing," came the terse response.

"Then why the security and bodyguards?"

"Oh, come on," Simone said condescendingly, "It's the Balkans, anybody who's rich and has a family will have some form of security."

I shrugged; she was right.

Simone asked how much someone had been willing to pay to have him killed, so I told her, understanding the reasoning behind the question.

"Merde, that much! Someone really wants him out of the way."

I agreed, but the reason for the contract niggled me. Why? If he was who Simone said he was, why did someone want to take him out and why the false information in the contract?

"I suspect his business may gave connections to some dodgy corners of the world. Why wasn't this all checked?" I mused and then – like a lightning bolt we both reached the same conclusion – the broker was in on it! Which would account for him having seemingly dropped off the face of the earth, I'd been trying to contact him to no avail.

"Look, keep digging for me – usual terms and a bonus for your team. Two days." I ended the call and, staring into the flames of the fire, I'd began planning my next moves. If the Broker was playing games with me, I needed to find out why and deal with the fallout, and if he wasn't working alone, who was behind all of this?

After a cold night, I'd trudged through the woods and commenced the arduous task of finding and safeguarding the explosive charges placed the previous day. The three at the base of the overhang were quickly dealt with. The problem was the one I had decided at the last moment to place in the snow ridge above the outcrop. It had taken me four hours to find the damn thing, and that was only by accident. Removing the detonators, and the Semtex was no more dangerous than modelling clay.

Returning to my overnight camp, I cleared up the evidence of my stay. I checked out the chalet one last time and, with a new perspective, I realised that what I previously believed to be covered garden furniture was children's play equipment. I'd fallen into the trap of believing what I had expected to see, not what was really there. The anger bubbling beneath the surface grew at the evidence of being duped; someone would pay.

After stashing my weapons and the explosives in a secure location, one of many I maintained around the world, I drove through the night to a safe house in Venice. It was an apartment in a 17th-century building overlooking the Grand Canal with the Basilica Santa Maria della Salute in the distance. An attractive apartment with a beautiful view that did nothing to abate my sour mood.

I had been tricked into almost killing a seemingly innocent man and his family, and I wanted to know why. Plus, I needed to make someone pay, if it ever got out that I could be manipulated, work would dry up. My anger at my gullibility was physical, as the several dents in the irreplaceable wallpaper in my bedroom could attest.

My contracts came through one of several brokers I trusted to work through. Brokers ensured anonymity to all parties. That there were a dozen or so premier brokers active had surprised me when I was first forced to become an independent contractor. Previously, work had come from my government agency.

The contract that triggered this situation didn't come from one of my usual three, but I had used this Broker in the past. I prefer not to know where the contract originated: that's why brokers are used as a cutout. Only now did I need to see if it was the contractee, the Broker, or possibly both, who'd fed me false information, which was proving difficult as the Broker had disappeared. Which in itself was telling.

Then, after two days, Simone had a breakthrough. There'd been a knock on the door, and a breathless Simone scurried inside, closing and locking the door behind her. She was one of a small handful who knew the location of the apartment. She was a petite, attractive, dark-haired Parisian beauty, the smile she gave me lit up her face.

"The broker is dead," she told me, after giving me a long hug, which achieved its goal of leaving me breathless. "I'm fairly sure he was the patsy in this setup."

"Why do you think that?" I said after regaining my composure.

"There's a rumour that a contractor was hired to silence the Broker before you could get to him. His body was discovered in his car, and his office was burnt to the ground, which suggests there was information that could identify who was behind this."

"It must be obvious to the client I've failed to complete the assignment. If they have any sense, they will know the reason why. But hopefully not that I intend to hold them accountable for putting innocent children at risk."

"And you want me to discover who that is," Simone responded, "for you to explain the error of their ways."

"Forcefully," I agreed.

Simone had spent the rest of the day on her phone and

laptop, delving deeply into the life and death of the deceased Broker, interspersed with forays into the business dealings of Marko's companies. I contributed by ensuring her coffee cup was topped up and the snack bowls were replenished.

She looked up after a couple of hours, "I know who took the contract on the broker." She named a second-tier assassin who had a reputation as being completely unscrupulous and somewhat sloppy.

"And who hired him?"

"It didn't come through any broker I know," she said adamantly. "None of them would accept a contract on one of their own; it would open up too many cans of worms. They were invaluable in identifying the Assassin, and all insisted it had to have been an independent contract."

I had agreed. "Open season on brokers would be a nightmare."

"True, so much so they've put a price on the assassin's head, I doubt he'll be still breathing this time tomorrow."

"That will teach him to bite the hand that feeds him. But that doesn't help me find out who hired me?"

"I doubt he ever knew, but I'm so much better. Just a couple more calls and I'll have it," she gloated.

An hour later, she danced around the apartment, singing, "I'm so good."

She gave me a satisfied grin. "You can't hide from the keyboard queen," she boasted.

I gave Simone her due and let her praise herself for a few minutes before demanding an explanation.

"I think I know the who and the why," she teased, giving me a coy smile that would have made me go weak under normal circumstances.

Trying and failing to hide my exasperation, I asked. "And that would be?"

"Have you ever heard of a Finnish company called Impi Industrial Consortium, or its chairman, Eero Heikkinen?"

I thought about it, but neither name rang a bell. "No," I admitted.

"He was behind that hit in Madrid."

Now that one I did recall. I'd needed to be very inventive for that contract. The corporate jet with the company's CEO and finance director had left Madrid for New York and several hours later had disappeared over the Atlantic.

An immaculately forged pass and work order had given me access to the plane. A rigged pressurisation valve and alarm system and a sabotaged emergency air system had done the job. The cabin had slowly depressurised mid-flight, and the crew and passengers had been starved of Oxygen. The jet followed the autopilot's instructions, finally running out of fuel after failing to land in the Azores to refuel.

"I remember that one," I'd told her. In fact, that had been the first of several similar contracts over a year from the same Broker.

Simone nodded, "It seems that when rival companies threaten his operations, he believes that legal options are ineffectual. Eero's corporate strategy is to permanently remove the senior management of those companies."

"And you think the hit on Marko and his family was part of this strategy."

"My research shows that the two companies are contending for several extremely lucrative contracts in the far east. Business insiders believe that Marko's personality is the chief reason why his group is the preferred option for almost all of them. If Impi fails to win the majority, the group will suffer financially, and Eero's position will come under extreme pressure. I doubt if he will survive."

I'd nodded in understanding. "So Eero has reverted to his old standby and is now trying to remove his rival company's figurehead and disrupt their bidding process."

"Yes," replied Simone.

"And he doesn't care who else gets caught up in his mess," I responded angrily. "I think Mr. Heikkinen and I need to discuss the error of his ways in person."

Simone gave me a calculated look. "Would you like me to find out where he is?"

"Is the Pope catholic? Of course." Then I considered my options and added aggressively. "Get the word out that I will take it extremely personally if anyone else were to accept a contract on Marko; he's protected until I say otherwise."

A few unwise amateurs might briefly consider trying for the payday until the facts of life were explained, but none of the professionals would, nor would their brokers. I'd bought Marko a temporary reprieve; now I had to make it permanent by removing the source of the contract, while removing the stain on my honour.

Locating Eero hadn't been difficult; he and his family lived on an estate a hundred kilometres north of Tampere in Finland. Unfortunately finding an opportune moment to have a quiet conversation without his ever-present security interfering was proving to much harder After a week, there was had been a glimmer of light.

Which all explained why I was currently having to explain to Santa the facts of life, or preferably his impending death, the choice solely dependent upon the level of his cooperation. I spoke in Finnish, so there would be no confusion. While I offered him his options, I busied myself fixing his dislocated finger and forced the hand into his glove.

The other, more pertinent reason was that Eero's company headquarters had reserved the winter wonderland to celebrate the winter solstice. The event was family-orientated, and the security checks were restricted to the compound's entrances. So far, a steady stream of proud parents and sticky children had been visiting Santa's chalet, but not yet the one person I was looking forward to most.

Eero was a widower with two grown-up married daughters and three young grandchildren. The children, who called Eero Grandpop, were his Achilles heel; the ruthless business magnate was a teddy bear around them.

Now you understand why one of the world's deadliest assassins was dressed in the pornographic elf's costume. Wondering if there was something in the local water that turned dry Finish men into groping octopuses. I fended off the umpteenth hand that had brushed my leg without permanently removing the offending limb, restricting my response to grinding my pointed heel into his foot.

His wife ushered their children, clutching their presents, from the glorified shed that had been turned into a cartoonish toy workshop. The husband followed, limping and gave me a baleful, hurt look.

"What are you waiting for?" Santa wheezed, looking anxious. His eyes were wildly flicking around the room, vainly hoping for salvation. I crushed it by pointing out to him my small silenced Twenty-two. Santa fell silent, pushing himself back on his throne, revealing the damp patch from when he had pissed himself.

I hushed him, hearing the next group approaching the cabin.

"Just remember," I told him. "Act naturally and you will come out of this alive. Try to warn anyone; the first bullet will be for you."

I was getting anxious, but finally Eero was in the last group to enter the chalet. I guess he ensured that all his underlings saw him playing the caring boss.

His daughters ushered the grandchildren over to Santa, who, after a brief glance in my direction, played his role as though his life depended on it, which it did. Eero stood back, fulfilling the role of benign and doting grandfather perfectly.

I retrieved the presents his PA had dropped off; the common presents were unsuitable for his little angels. I had a special gift for Eero that I slipped into the top of my right boot.

I had debated long and hard over the nature of Eero's fate. A bullet or knife seemed too merciful. He needed to suffer for a long time, and I had the perfect solution. A drug cocktail I had an ex-East German doctor create. There is a medical condition known as 'locked-in syndrome.' The mind stays active, aware of everything that goes on around it. But it can no longer control the body. The person appears to be in a coma. That is what the first part of the cocktail mimics, the effect slowly wearing off after six months.

The second drug is what would ultimately cause Eero's death.

It was a compound that permanently affected the body's pain receptors. Making them more than a hundred times more sensitive.

Imagine the situation, unable to move, fully aware of your surroundings and in constant agony. Could my revenge be any better? By the time the paralytic agent wore off, Eero would be a gibbering madman, begging to be put out of his misery.

The children accepted their gifts with happy laughter. Santa wished them good health and a Merry Christmas. I ushered the family out, ensuring Eero would be the last to leave.

I offered him season greetings, moving closer to give him a hug. He did what any red-blooded male who felt secure in his surroundings would do when approached by an attractive elf: he returned the hug. The needle slid unerringly into the vein in his neck, and the plunger depressed. The anaesthetic agent knocked him out almost immediately, then I injected him with the cocktail, and I let him slide to the ground. The deed was done.

Santa gave a half-strangled gasp, starting to rise. A second dose of anaesthesia, and Santa was artfully arranged on his throne with an almost empty bottle of pepper vodka in his lap.

I stepped to the door and called out loudly in a scared voice, "Help, I need help here; he's collapsed." Hearing anxious voices coming close, I slipped out the rear door and faded into the darkness.

Within an hour, I was at the bar in the Ice Hotel, enjoying a drink with the off-duty receptionist who had caught my eye earlier. I hung around for several more days enjoying her company, until I heard that Eero had been transferred to a private clinic in Helsinki. Before I left Finland, I took pleasure in paying him a clandestine visit, sneaking into his room in the early hours of the morning while the nurse on duty was dosing at her desk. There was an immense sense of satisfaction in seeing the terror in his eyes grow as I outlined his fate for the rest of his life, and why he was suffering this fate.

Eero only managed to last for several days after he finally regain control of his bodily functions. Choosing the cowards way by overdosing on the OxyContin that his physicians prescribed in a vain attempt to ease his pain.

His rambling suicide note cursed the unknown woman who had done this to him. Even now he was unable to accept it had been his criminal business practices that had caused his downfall. Usually I keep in the shadows, this time I was willing to let Simone spread the rumour that I had been behind Eero's painful demise. Enforcing the understanding that I would do the same to anyone who put me in the same situation. This only added to my reputation as a person you didn't want to cross, and the legend of Verity the Assassin grew throughout the underworld faster than Santa Claus delivered presents on Christmas Eve.

Andrew H Martin's debut novel, an action thriller, Living Proof, is available from Amazon and selected retailers worldwide. Andrew is currently writing the sequel which will be released in late 2026 or early 2027.

She Felt Like Home

By Carol Leyland

When life gives you lemons, you make lemonade, or so the saying goes, but due to the British climate, Lucy couldn't grow them in her allotment. She did, however, have punnets of strawberries she'd bought at the supermarket, which she was cutting into delicate slivers to put on top of the pavlova she'd made for her best friend Pam's birthday party that evening.

So far, it'd been a normal Friday. Work had been quiet, giving her baking time, so she nearly sliced off the top of her finger when her phone rang with an unknown number. 'Shit,' she said, dropping both the strawberry and knife, which ricocheted onto the floor scarily close to her little toe.

Answering cautiously, 'Hello?' Hoping they'd ring off or say 'wrong number.'

'Lucy? It's Jean.'

My heart sank. Was the party cancelled, or had they planned a different surprise for their friend? God, she hoped not, it had taken everyone long enough to decide on the pavlova and where to hold the party.

'Oh God, Lucy, I don't know how to say this. I can't believe it. We were in the taxi, Pam and I, we were going to the hairdressers, and she just... died.' Her voice cracked as she said it. Jean had known Pam since school, and fifty years is a very long time for a friendship. 'One minute she was talking and laughing, the next she was just... gone.'

'Hell, that's awful. Poor Pam. Poor you. Are you okay? I'm so sorry. Is there anything I can do?' Lucy said, struggling to find the right words, so many came cascading from her mouth.

'We were laughing about her getting a purple rinse to celebrate turning sixty when it looks like her heart just gave out. The driver and I tried everything, but she was just gone.'

They had all known about Pam being in heart failure, but she had carried on and had more vitality than many of her friends who were half her age.

'I don't know what to say, I'm so sorry, what should we do about tonight…. her party…. Is it too late to cancel? People have been coming in from all over.'

'I've got the list of who's coming, can we split it and call people?' suggested Jean. 'I'll go down to the Deer Park just in case anyone doesn't get the call. There was so much to do at the hospital, or I'd have called earlier,' her voice unsteady. Jean was stoic and never cracked, but today, on the phone, her voice was wobbly, and she stumbled over her words.

'Of course, send me half and I'll do what I can.'

'Thanks, will email it over. God, what an awful day.'

And with a click, Jean hung up.

Lucy stood looking down at the pavlova, Pam's favourite. The tears began to fall gently at first, then erupted into a tsunami down her face until she was sobbing uncontrollably, holding onto the work surface for support. Why was life so cruel?

Pam was a dream of a friend, funny, kind, helpful and full of the best kind of advice. She'd been a mutual supportive scaffold for the past few years as they both went through separations and divorces and tried to forge life as older lesbians in a young person's world.

'What will I do without her?' sobbed Lucy.

Jean's email arrived, and she managed to reach most people. She left messages for others to stay away and asked them to call her, a strategy that was surprisingly successful. At the bottom of the list was Elizabeth.

Now Elizabeth was an enigma. Pam had told her the story many times. How she and Elizabeth had fallen in love at university thirty-five years ago, a love that was not to be, as Elizabeth had married a man to conform to the wishes of her parents, and over time, they had both lost touch. Now here Lucy was with her number in her hand, the butterflies doing cartwheels in her stomach. She wasn't sure why, but the idea of talking to the woman whom Pam had never forgotten made her nervous. Lucy dialled, her hand slightly shaking.

'Elizabeth? My name's Lucy, I'm a friend of Pam's.'

'Oh, hi. Is something wrong?'

She took a deep breath. 'I'm so sorry, and I hate to tell you this on the phone, but Pam died this morning. We're trying to let everyone know before they set off for her party. It's been such a shock.'

There was silence down the line; she could hear heavy breathing and what sounded like a sob.

'I know she'd been ill for some time; I don't know what to say, but thanks for telling me. I'm staying at The Village; I travelled up today from Somerset. Is there anything I can do?' asked Elizabeth, her voice cracking down the line.

'I don't think so, but thanks for offering.' Then an urge took hold of Lucy, and she asked, 'Do you want to come over? I'm not far from there.'

'Are you sure?'

'Of course, you've come all this way, in case you want company?'

'That would be lovely, just message me your address. As long as you're sure.'

Not quite believing what she'd just done, Lucy texted her address and then looked in the bathroom mirror after washing her tear-stained face. Lucy felt even more nervous now. Her butterflies appeared to be stomping on her heart, making it beat out of her chest. She was going to meet the woman who had stolen the heart of her friend all those years ago.

Half an hour later, a dark green mini pulled up outside and parked askew on the road outside. As she got out of the car, she realised that Elizabeth was not at all how she'd imagined. She was a small-framed, grey-haired, athletic woman, dressed in khaki trousers, a white shirt, and small red shoes. She opened the boot, got out a bunch of flowers and a hessian bag, and then walked purposefully to the door, holding out her hand as she got closer.

'I'm so pleased to meet you, Lucy. Thank you for inviting me over.'

'My pleasure. Come in, I'm glad to meet you finally.'

'You too, I've so many questions I want to ask about Pam. I don't know how much you know about our… friendship. She meant such a lot to me at one time.'

'Would you like a drink? Coffee, tea? You've had such a long day.'

Elizabeth went into her bag and brought out a carton of oat milk.

'I brought my own if that's ok. I'd love a coffee if that's ok.'

They sipped coffee with oat milk, sharing stories - happy ones, sad ones, ones filled with tears, and others that brought laughter.

'I loved Pam you know. I hope she knew that. I just felt trapped, trying to do the right thing by everyone,' explained Elizabeth, her head lowered.

'Doing it right for everyone but yourself Elizabeth,' replied Lucy.

'True. But times were different then, and I didn't want to disappoint my parents. I knew I would lose everything if I'd stayed with Pam. I didn't have the strength.'

'I do understand, I've heard so many women with similar stories. You aren't alone. But you've had a happy life?'

Elizabeth looked sad. 'I had good times, having the children, working, being able to work in a male-dominated world. But there was something missing; I always knew that. I'm just sorry I never got to see Pam again.'

'I understand that, but she knew you were coming, didn't she, as you were on the party list?'

'She messaged me out of the blue and told me about her big birthday, and I wanted to come and see her. Reminisce maybe. We swapped a few messages beforehand and think she was glad I was coming.'

'I'm sure that she was, Elizabeth. She was such a wonderful woman, wasn't she?

Within an hour, it felt like they'd known each other for years. Coffee drinking turned into wine, along with the pavlova, accompanied by toasts in honour of Pam. Pasta was cooked and eaten, hours flying by as the light turned to dark. The moon shone through the windows, creating a warm glow in the living room, lit by candles.

Elizabeth, returning from the bathroom, sat closer on the sofa, their hands almost touching as she did so; a spark shot from one to the other, making them both jump. Their eyes met, and a flash of attraction they'd been denying for the past few hours shook the atmosphere in the room.

Lucy thought, *'I'm an intelligent woman, but I've made many mistakes. Becoming involved with a married woman was not high on the agenda of good things to do right now.'* Absolute gay panic.

Elizabeth took her hand, rubbing her thumb on the back of it, their eyes meeting again. She leaned in for a kiss, and the heat between them could have warmed a small town. Lucy pulled away.

'I can't, you're married. You're lovely, but I just can't. I'm sorry.

'I'm an idiot, I'm sorry. Pam would be so disappointed in me,' said Elizabeth, pulling back.

'No, she wouldn't. Aren't you happy in your marriage?'

'I don't know. I've hidden who I am for so long, I don't know who I am anymore,' said Elizabeth, standing up, tears in her pretty hazel eyes. 'I'd better go; I've made such a fool of myself.'

And with that, she shot out of the front door to her car before Lucy had a chance to stop her. The little green Mini turned around and headed off down the street.

Lucy closed the front door as the car lights dimmed into the distance. Where on earth had all that come from? Was it the grief of losing Pam? Was it really an attraction? She'd been single for so long she'd forgotten how it felt to want someone again. Grief, that must be what it had been for them both. It hits you sideways when you least expect it, and it weighs than you would think. That was it, grief, Lucy convinced herself.

After speaking to Jean, who confirmed that everyone from the party had been told Lucy went to bed, feeling slightly drunk and more than a little confused. She was so sad that Pam had died; she would never see her friend again. However, meeting Elizabeth made her feel like a gift had been given to her amidst the sadness.

Over the following days, Jean took charge, as she often did, as she was the executor of Pam's Will. Pam, as predicted had written out her funeral instructions down to the tiniest detail. The readings, the songs and the lovely greenfield site where a tree would be planted at a later date to grow out of the goodness and kindness that was her. Between them, they messaged and called everyone who needed to know. Lucy sent a message to Elizabeth because there was no reply to her call, informing her of the date and time and that she would be welcome to the Wake afterwards. She stressed that, due to the distance involved, if she was unable to attend, she was sure Pam would understand.

As the days went by, Elizabeth didn't reply to the message, and Lucy felt sad that she didn't feel able to stay in touch. She didn't want her to feel embarrassed or that she had made a fool of herself, but she didn't know how to reach out to her, just in case her husband answered the call. The last thing she wanted to do was to cause her any further pain.

The day of the funeral arrived. The weather was horrid, a solid drizzle had been streaming from the sky for days, and as she got out of her car and put up her umbrella, she couldn't see far in front of her as she headed towards the chapel that was close to the greenfield site. Lucy had taken a wrong turning, so she was running late as she rushed from the car to the chapel.

Inside the door were a stack of folded umbrellas of assorted colours, as well as Wellington boots. Lucy kicked herself for not wearing hers. Her sensible shoes had already let in water from the walk from the car.

Pam's instructions had told everyone to wear something colourful, so Lucy was wearing a knee-length red dress with a black wide belt around her waist. She wished, once in the cold chapel, that she had opted for warmth over fashion.

All of Pam's friends were there, a mixture of smiles with sad eyes, all waiting for the humanist that had been personally chosen to begin. She scoured the pews and saw a space at the back with some women whom she'd met before on a writing course. After saying quick hellos, the humanist attracted their attention and began the most beautiful service Lucy had ever attended.

The readings were full of the warmth of the achievements in Pam's life, of which there were many, some of which it was clear people didn't know about. She had lived a full life, albeit cut short, and packed a great deal into it.

After the final song was played, six of her friends carried her from the chapel to her recently dug grave, all of them scurrying to put on boots and retrieve umbrellas as fast as they could. The rain had stopped, which was a relief, but the grass was sodden and muddy in places as they picked their way across the field to Pam's final resting place. As they gathered around the grave, Jean read out a final poem, and then the wicker basket coffin was lowered into the ground. This is when the tears really fell, to the point that she couldn't see as her eyes stung from her mascara, which had melted onto her eyes and down her face. Everyone began to file back to their cars to drive to the Wake at the pub closest to the chapel, but Lucy had to sort herself out before she could safely drive. So slowly heading back to her car, head down, following the blur of people ahead, she didn't notice a woman who fell into step beside her. It wasn't until she spoke that Lucy realised who it was. Elizabeth.

'Lucy,' she said. Lucy slightly stumbled, and Elizabeth took her elbow and helped her back to her car. 'Are you okay?'

'Yes, it was a lovely service, wasn't it. Excuse me, I need to get something from my car,' said Lucy, going into her glove compartment and retrieving some wet wipes, which she used on her face to remove the black streaks.

Suddenly, the heavens opened again, and Elizabeth was caught in the deluge without an umbrella in sight.

'Get in,' said Lucy, scooting over to the driver's seat.

Elizabeth got in and closed the door, her short grey hair flat to her head, the rainwater dripping down onto her black coat.

They sat in silence for a few minutes, the car slowly steaming up the longer they sat.

'I'm sorry if I've made things awkward, I didn't mean to...,' said Elizabeth.

'It's fine. It's been harder today than I ever thought it would be. I can't believe I won't ever see Pam again. She was a special woman.'

'She really was. Are you going to the Wake?'

'I am, now I can see again. Are you?' asked Lucy, looking over at Elizabeth for the first time. She had lost weight since she'd last seen her.

'I'd like to. I don't know where it is.'

'Follow me if that'd help. It's not far,' said Lucy helpfully. Her insides were overcome again with the same butterflies she'd had when she first met Elizabeth, which was ridiculous. She was a menopausal woman, not a teenager. It had been a year since anyone had affected her like this.

'Look before we go, I need to tell you something. I've not stopped thinking about you since I went home. I have been more certain about myself than I ever have. I've told my husband I'm gay and I've left him. Losing Pam and the wasted years is all the push I needed.'

'Oh hell, Elizabeth, that's huge. Are you sure?'

'I have never been more certain. I packed my things and came up for the funeral, and I'm not going back. We haven't really had a marriage for many years, and he knows that. I know I can't carry on with the charade anymore.'

'Where will you go? What will you do?' I asked.

'I'm renting a cottage for a couple of weeks whilst I find somewhere to go. I feel freer than I have in years. I hope I haven't made an idiot of myself.'

'Not at all. It's a brave thing you've done. What will you do now?'

'I don't know, recover, I suppose and do some work on finding who I am'.

'Sounds like a good plan. But don't be hard on yourself. You've done the tricky bit now, take your time, don't rush into anything.'

'Like fall in love', said Elizabeth, looking deep into my eyes.

'Especially that. Take your time, there's no rush,' said Lucy. The memories of her years of relationship disasters were at the forefront of her memory.

'I'd like to see you again, would that be ok?'

'Of course, I'd like that, but as friends, you've got enough going on.'

'Thank you, Lucy. The relief feels huge. Let's go to the Wake. I want to hear more stories about Pam.'

'Great, get your car and follow me down to the pub,' said Lucy, her insides quaking with everything Elizabeth had told her. 'Keep your cool, woman,' she said to herself as she drove to the Wake.

The Wake was what everyone needed: a chance to talk about their friend and to say goodbye with tears and laughter. Elizabeth chatted with many people, her eyes sparkling as she learned more about her friend's life in the years since she'd last seen her. By the end of the afternoon, everyone parted ways, feeling both sad and relieved to have been able to let out some of their grief. Elizabeth waved to Lucy as she left and shortly afterwards sent a text saying she'd be in touch soon.

Over the following weeks, they met for coffee, for meals, and for cinema visits. Laughing and crying, having misunderstandings and falling out, but falling back in again shortly after. Elizabeth quickly found a flat, a part-time job, and volunteer work. Even though she thought everything would go wrong, her life was going right.

'It's because you're living your best life now, that's why it's all coming together,' Lucy had reassured her when she felt low, or her divorce letters brought her down.

Time ticked on, and they saw each other twice a week, chatting on the phone every day for hours when they didn't meet up. Conversations from her gardening experiences and getting an exclusive allotment near Lucy's despite a long waiting list, as well as talks about archaeology and history, and projects Elizabeth had volunteered for and secured coveted places. Her life really was on the up.

Lucy's, however, was static. Romantic feelings were getting in the way of their friendship. Slowly, she realised how she longed to see her. Longed for the chance for another moment on the sofa where they would look into each other's eyes, but this time she would kiss her and say I love you and nothing would stop her. However, the moment they'd shared was never mentioned again. The 'let's be friends' had been taken on board, and she'd respected Lucy's boundaries. However, she didn't want her to respect them anymore.

Christmas was approaching. A time of year that Lucy dreaded most. She'd lost both of her parents, both before and after it, and she'd always felt lost when it came to BIG DAY because of how happy she was supposed to feel, but in reality, she just wanted to hide. These feelings she'd shared with Elizabeth a few weeks earlier during a particularly drunken lunch.

On Christmas Eve, Elizabeth arranged to meet Lucy at the allotment on the pretence of collecting the sprout stalks for the following few days. It was a cold day as she parked her car and walked down the makeshift pathway to where she could see Elizabeth waiting. Her wild grey head bobbed up and down in the distance as she had already set to cutting the stalks. Seeing me, she stood up and waved in greeting.

'Come look at my sprouts, aren't they the best you've ever seen? I've been so lucky getting this spot.'

'They are brilliant, you've enough to feed the 5000.'

'Are you okay? You look odd.'

'Do I?' said Lucy, her heart beating so hard in her chest she thought Elizabeth must be able to hear it too.

'You look like you need a hug?'

Elizabeth held her arms out wide, and Lucy allowed her to wrap herself around her. She smelled earthy with a hint of floral, and she stayed there a little longer than she intended. Pulling back, she avoided her gaze, but Elizabeth took her hand, brought it to her lips and kissed it. She couldn't hold back anymore and leaned in to kiss her. This time, neither of them resisted; they both were in the right place, at the right time. It was soft and delicious, just as Lucy had imagined it to be.

'Take me home,' said Elizabeth. So that's just what Lucy did as the first snow of winter fell on them as they walked hand in hand into their futures.

Carol Leyland is a short story writer for Provoco and has self-published two other novels.

Golden Threaded Pants

By Nicholas Vaughan

As I stepped through an archway at security an alarm went off, *Shoot*, I thought. The guard steered me to one side and waved his wand for conducting searches over me.

'It must be the gold in his label that's triggered it off.'

I replied, 'If I had gold sewn into the threads of my trousers all my worldly problems would be solved.'

The guard said, 'We must take you to do a more in-depth search.'

He led me to another room. The man said, 'My names Trevor, but we'll have to wait for the police to arrive so they can conduct the search.'

'Okay.' I replied.

After two hours the police arrived.

'I'm Officer Evans and we'll be searching for drugs and dangerous weapons.'

He made me stand against a wall. The officer ran his hands up and down my body and cried out, 'I can feel something! It must be in his pants.'

He stuck one hand up my trouser leg. Another officer stepped forward to assist. Evans tugged with all his might. Without warning, a length of gold thread unravelled from my trousers. Evans pulled at it.

'Have you got something that we can wind this thread onto?'

The officer and Trevor went off and came back several minutes later with a spinning wheel.

Evans said, 'Set it up, then.'

Before long, they had it in operation. As the wheel spun, it slowly but surely unwound the thread from my trousers leaving me dressed only in my birthday suit. The officer could see I was embarrassed, so he gave me a three peaked hat to cover my modesty.

Trevor waved his wand over me. I disappeared. A second later, I reached another dimension. A lamp was stood on the floor before me, and out of it Elzbieta appeared and spoke.

'You get three wishes. Don't waste them!'

I thought long and hard about it.

I said, 'Can I have a new pair of Turkish golden pants?'

Elzbieta clicked its fingers, and a pair of trousers appeared. I proceeded to put them on. The minute they were on, I was blinded by the gleaming gold on my pants. I put my hands to my eyes and cried out in pain.

Elzbieta said, 'That wasn't the best of choices? Why don't you opt for something different?'

I thought hard again.

'Can I have something that will allow me to gain worldly riches.'

A man stood before me.

I said, 'Who is this?'

'This man's body is riddled with cancer. By looking after him, you'll learn to appreciate the small things.'

I looked horrified.

'Won't I catch a hideous disease from the man?'

Elzbieta replied, 'Don't be daft. It's not infectious.'

I nodded my head and approached the man.

'What's your name?'

'I'm Ben,' he said.

'I'm Nick.'

I said, 'I'll get you scrubbed up first, then we can go out and have a slap-up meal.'

Ben replied, 'I'd appreciate a good wash, but not the meal so much.'

'Of course, I'm sorry, that was insensitive of me.'

Ben said, 'If I can spend time with people doing normal things, that might help me to forget what I'm going through.'

I replied, 'Let's go and get you cleaned up.'

In the corner, there was a bath carved out of the rock. I turned a tap and clean water flowed out. I helped to undress

Ben and assisted him to clean himself. I picked up a loofah and passed it to him.

Ben said, 'Scrub my back with that.'

Once he was done, I pulled down a towel, passed it to Ben and waited.

Ben said, 'Do you have a spare outfit that I can wear?'

'No, only the clothes on my back, but I don't mind sharing those with you.'

'That's so generous of you. All I normally get is unkindness as people think they can catch what I have. That's nonsense.'

I took off my sweater, then pulled the T-Shirt off my back. I passed it to Ben.

I said, 'I've already lost my trousers. Otherwise, I'd happily give them to you.'

Ben replied, 'I totally understand that. It's been such a joy being able to share the small things in life with you. It's made me realise that I have more to give.'

'Really?'

'Yes, I can share moments of my life's history.'

I said, 'For my own part, it's been a pleasure sharing all of this with you. And its taught me the most important lesson in life.'

'And that is?'

I said, 'That one must always make time for others.'

I stepped closer to Ben and embraced him for several minutes. Whilst we hugged, I could hear him sob quietly. *This poor man*, I thought, *his life is about to end.*

There was a flash and the man disappeared. I was left stood with Elzbieta again.

'You've only got one wish left, use it wisely!'

I gazed searchingly upwards.

'Perhaps, you could give me a security guards wand for conducting searches.'

Elzbieta said, 'That's an odd choice. Still, I'll have a go.'

A moment later a wand hung in the air. I walked up to it, and it dropped into my hand. I took the wand and ran it up and down my body.

'No,' shouted out Elzbieta, 'if you do that you'll disappear!'

A moment later, I resurfaced in another world.

I said, 'Where am I?'

Trevor replied, 'You're at an airport going through security.'

'No,' I said. 'I've been trying to get away from this place all day.'

Trevor replied, 'Did you make your millions whilst you were away?'

I said, 'No, but I gained something that's far more valuable and positive.'

Trevor looked at me with a baffled expression.

'Are you off your rocker!?!'

I said, 'I may have lost my golden threaded Turkish pants, but now I've learnt something that can be used in all spheres of life.'

Trevor replied, 'I'm impressed, but I think I'd rather take the money.'

Nicholas Vaughan's debut novel, The Unwrapping is now available from Amazon and selected retailers worldwide.

Mrs Guy Fawkes

By Emma Hardy

I cannot believe that bastard has roped me in on this.

'They'll never suspect a woman,' he said, stroking the red bristles on his chin.

So here I am, cowering in a corner praying, quite literally, that no one spots this flicker that reflects as a shadow on the wall behind me.

I never thought I'd set foot in this building. I can taste the damp which engulfs my mouth, making it hard to swallow. The stench of sweat is in the air; I suspect my husband is drowning in his own sweat in this moment too. Selfish man hasn't considered how I may get out without the light.

It's nearly time to move. I have no way to know for sure which way I'm going.

'Follow your nose,' he said.

There are endless routes I could take. Grey tunnels lead off in different directions every time I turn. He seems so sure about this plan.

I tread carefully; my eyes need to be everywhere. I push open a door. Of course it squeaks. I quicken my pace. Voices echo in a low murmur. Then a laugh. I recognise it instantly. Him. My husband. The traitor.

I have a few more doors to go. His laugh keeping me right, leading me like a trail of crumbs along the way.

I see him. He looks at his men. A couple of servants he grabbed from a nearby village.

'I told you all I had the most loyal wife.'

I shiver. It's only when I stop, I realise just how much the cold has caught my breath down here.

He plants a kiss on my cheek and takes the lantern from me. My line of sight now feels blinded, as much as my dim husband's judgement. I see the boys bow down to me as silhouettes. I remain silent, staring. Time to get out as fast as my legs will carry me. I cannot stay to witness whatever our fate has sealed. I will likely never see my husband again.

The next part of my plan that evening, he knows nothing about. A few days ago, I took some of his clothes and adjusted them to make them fit my slender frame. I found a quiet alleyway nearby to store them before I went into the cellars. I know it will not do to be a woman of my status lurking around London at this ungodly hour. I have no choice but to disguise myself as a man. In darkness, I slither out of my lantern clothing, pull up my husband's breeches, tug down a shirt and drape myself in one of his cloaks. My old clothes can get left behind. I don't recognise the person that wore them anymore. I sit and wait as I watch the Houses of Parliament from a safe distance, whilst ensuring I can see absolutely everything.

I think back to how we met. A mutual friend encouraged us to dance at one of her parties- and then came the letters. What a charmer. He'd dazzle, and swoon, and tell me his inner most thoughts. Yet, I couldn't shake the feeling he was writing the same letter to at least four other women, maybe five. He insisted not. Then, one night, he knocked on the door, with a bottle of the finest Scottish whisky for my father, and I agreed to his modest proposal. Perhaps I'd got him wrong after all. We had a lavish wedding. He tells me he's never known such a spark between two people. I rolled my eyes. His obsession for fire had already begun. A line formed around us. I had no idea he had so many friends. One by one, his men came to wish us well and I thought the line would never end. Then came the dancing. And the beer. I can't help but smile when I think of that. The day I fell in love with my husband. It was a shame it didn't last.

My thoughts are rudely interrupted by a rat which rushes past my feet. I then realise that I've been sat here for some time now and there has been no movement from the Houses of Parliament. I like London at this time of night and must do this more often. I realise how much more comfortable men's clothes are to mine and how invisibility feels as no one has challenged why I am sat here or acted inappropriately towards me. It is astonishing how liberating it feels to be a man. I wrap my cloak around me tighter.

I see what looks like an army of men entering the Houses of Parliament. They move fast. I wonder if this is the moment. There has thus far been no explosion, no noise, so my husband and his helpers clearly haven't made the onward journey in the cellar to the explosives yet.

I remember reading a book in the adjoining room to his friends at our house as they excited themselves, detailing the plan. It churned my stomach. I pretended not to hear. Then, in bed that same evening, he relayed it all to me. I didn't want to know and told him so. But he went into detail about how positive it will all be, for our lives, our status, our future. I almost believed him. He talked to me about the lantern, and I got so swept away in his passion that I agreed. It's only when I woke the next morning, I realised just how foolish he is, as am I for agreeing to join this desperate plan. He grew even more obsessed about gunpowder, fire, maps of the cellars, his military experience making him the perfect man for the job, he said. He was only fixated on this. Nothing else mattered to him. I went to bed alone every night after that. Within only months, I had lost my husband to the most idiotic plan in history.

Silence crawls all over me. I expected something to have happened by now, yet it could not be a more peaceful night. I have never known London so hollow. No light, no life. I take a deep breath in anticipation for what is to come. The moon stares down at me.

Then, it comes. They've found them. The royal guards drag out my husband and his conspirators out of the Houses of Parliament. I see him, dishevelled. The lantern is still being clasped in his hand. Its light has gone out. He is shouting, pleading with them to let him go. It has all been a mistake, he says. He is ignored. The other men are more physical and try and escape the clutches of the guards, to no avail. I edge closer to the action, and my husband stops and looks at me. I smile and he looks confused, then elbows the guard in the stomach but another guard hits him hard and I watch my husband fall to the ground defeated. I cannot stand to watch a second longer. It is time to go home.

As I reach my bedroom, I peel off the disguise and let my dark hair tumble down my back. I think I enjoyed being a man a bit too much. I know I will do it again. I climb into bed and stretch out my arms and legs wide. For the first time in my life, I can just be me. I think of my husband and wonder if he's reached the tower yet. I go to sleep on that thought.

I'm woken up by the paper boy shouting close to my window.

'Remember, remember the fifth of November, Gunpowder, treason, and plot. Read all about it, read all about it.'

I know it will be a day I never forget. I remember, too, that my husband hasn't come home. After getting dressed, I grab a paper from the boy and see what is being said. Knowing most of the story, I skim read looking for my husband's name.

'Guido Fawkes, aged 35 is now being imprisoned at the Tower, and will be questioned to name his co-conspirators in this barbaric plot to kill the King.'

He won't give the other's names, I know he won't. He always said he'd do this alone.

A knock at the door leaves me hiding the newspaper in the library between some books and I await my maid. I know who this will be and wipe my hands on my dress.

She shakes her head. 'Ma'am.' Some guards enter behind her. I must keep my composure.

'Welcome, gentlemen, what can I do for you?'

'I'm assuming you know that your husband is at the Tower?'

'Yes. Word travels fast.' I sit.

'We have to ask you, Mrs. Fawkes, did you know that your husband had thirty-six barrels of gunpowder stored not far from here, until only a couple of nights ago?'

I look up and they don't seem to know how to talk to me. If I were a man, they would be violent. But they are respectful to me as a woman, and my status. Even though my husband tried to kill the King.

'Thirty-six? Goodness, no. I am sorry. My husband kept himself to himself, I know absolutely nothing.' I cry, hoping I am convincing enough that they won't pursue any more questions.

'Do you know who his friends were?' They are softer this time.

'Not a clue, he'd swan off and leave me here alone, so I never saw them.' I grab my handkerchief and use it to cover my face. Disguises are serving me well at the moment.

'Sorry to have troubled you. But your husband will likely hang, so you might expect some suspicion.'

I nod, not knowing what to say. Perhaps I should have fallen to the ground, it would be more dramatic, but would it have been convincing? I do enough that they recognise my distress and walk out saying nothing further.

The next few days are a blur. People come and go, checking up on me, the husband who duped her wife as well as an attempted murderer. The worst kind. The story won't leave the papers. I stay in my library, comforted by other stories and ignoring the real life one I'm in. The knocking on the door is relentless.

That is, until the headline on day four.

'Guido names co-conspirators after enduring three days of torture.'

My immediate thoughts go to my husband being tortured. Then I remember what he did, tried to do, and read on. He's named them all. Stupid man. I never had him down as a grass. I read to the bottom of the page and for the first time I see it says that the guards were alerted after an anonymous letter was sent to the Palace to warn the King. I'm amazed that's at the bottom of the article. Surely that's bigger news? I continue to get word of the other men in the days that follow. I hear nothing from my husband. I am told by guards who visit me daily that I am not allowed to see him. My visitors soon trail off, not wanting to be associated with a traitor's wife. I pray to God every night, asking for his guidance at this lonely time.

Some of his friends have been shot dead. Some join him at the Tower. The torture drags for my husband, whom I have to remain loyal to, 'til death do us part.' I spend so much time alone, then dress up in my husbands altered clothing by night, where I feel free and can do as I please. I go into inns and have some beer; I can walk without being judged. I live my life in a new peaceful solitude.

The day finally comes. The day my husband will be hung, drawn and quartered. That morning, the guards tell me that I'm allowed to say my goodbyes. I will see him one last time as he reaches his death.

My father accompanies me, realising I should not go alone to the Tower. But he will leave us to talk, once inside. I walk in with my white gloves, and best earrings. I want him to see me looking as best I can, whilst I get ready to see my husband the worst he's ever looked. I am careful where I step, and do not brush against anything. It all feels tainted and dirty. I wish I could be a man walking through here. It'd be so much easier. Instead, I'm trembling, just wanting this over with.

I see a skeleton behind bars.

'Hello.'

I am not sure if I am at the correct cell, he is so unrecognisable. I turn to the guard, about to ask if I am at the right place but this bony creature whispers my name.

'Mary.'

His long, gingery beard has gone, his hair cropped. He is gaunt, pale and his eyes have gone black. Bruises are all over his body and are easy to see through his filthy white shirt. He stares at me, intently.

'I'm so sorry.'

I somehow keep my composure.

'It's quite all right.'

We sit for minutes in silence. Neither one knowing what else is to be said. We are strangers. Through the bars, he pokes my wedding ring.

'You are still wearing this.' He croaks.

I nod. I see he is not wearing his, but it doesn't matter to me. 'They took mine.'

I nod again.

He speaks one more time. 'I met the King.' He smirks.

I scowl at him for attempting to make a joke after everything he's put me through.

I turn my back, knowing the next time I see him, he'll be dying. The last conversation I'll ever have with my husband.

I say nothing to my father, as I already want that image of the shell of my husband out of my head. I fear the next event will be even harder to watch.

As I leave the Tower, the crowd has grown immeasurably. I am satisfied to linger near the back. I can't get too close to this. They bring out the men who my husband named as co-conspirators, but not him. One by one, the rope goes around their neck, and they lose their footing. The crowd jeer and throw their beers in the air in celebration. I turn to face my father as soon as I spot someone's insides on the floor. I cannot watch. These men suffer for so long that the sky has allowed darkness in the air. They have still not brought out my husband. I have a whole new pain still to come. I run off to be sick. I get pushed and shoved out the way as more onlookers come to see my husband. They chant his name with the word traitor. There's an unrecognisable pungent smell in the air. I never want to smell this stench ever again.

Then they bring him out, the crowd spirits lift, and the noise is piercing. My husband stoops as he's lead to his rope. He stares at his fellow dead friends, knowing what will be coming next. He looks around but can't seem to find what he's looking for. I cling to my father's shoulder, who looks expressionless. A few words are spoken and then he hangs. I watch as he tries to breathe but can't. The crowd again do a loud cheer, and a small bonfire is built on the edge on the crowd in celebration. I watch as the fire flickers, gets more ferocious and fuller of life, as my husband loses his. It crackles as his body parts are pulled out of his body. It burns the wood and gets stronger, and my husband's body gets weaker and slumps. As his body is further cut, more things are thrown on the fire which is now the wildest it's been. The smell of smoke clings to my lungs. It's all over.

Thank goodness my anonymous letter to the King was acknowledged and trusted to end this horrid affair. I prayed it had reached him in the days before. I walk away and smile as I am free to be the woman I want to be.

Emma Hardy's debut novel is releasing in early 2026

When It Was Christmas

By Jane Murray

Winter, unpleasant at the best of times, seemed to worsen with the passing of every year. This year, Luke thought, the winter they were experiencing was horrendous. He could not recall ever feeling so cold, he could not remember any previous winter that had started in late September and which, by March of the following year had still not abated, turning their days into an endless painful, frozen bleakness. The sky hung low and sullen, a dank grey overcoat for the thin grey gauze mist that was a permanent feature, an after effect of The Flash.

He was slumped in a miserable, frozen heap, a rough grey blanket wrapped around his thin frame, the coarseness of the material highlighting for him, the unrelenting toil of life now as opposed to his life *then*. Pulling his crudely fashioned chair closer to the fire, he threw on a couple more precious logs which he grabbed from the untidy pile on the floor in the corner and he rubbed his hands together, more miserable than he could ever remember being.

He was lucky enough to have a relic of past technology – a solar clock and calendar and despite everything that had happened since its manufacture, back in those long-ago days, it still worked. Like him, it had survived The Flash, the aftermath, the so-called nuclear winter and now, it told him that it was December the twenty-fourth. In another lifetime, it would have been Christmas Eve.

Outside, icicles hung bravely to the window lintels and Luke could see the whole landscape was coated in an icy white dusting of frost. God, if he still existed, knew what it was like for those who had to live underground, in their allocated pods. The death toll from this harsh winter would far exceed the deaths from any bloody virus, Luke thought. How ironic that they had fought so hard to prevent the spread of a man-made virus when in fact, nature was the real killer. The fire hissed and orange sparks spat from the glowing heart of the flames as a draught blew down the brick chimney.

As an Elite – after all, his father had been the Prime Minister of what used to be the United Kingdom – Luke and his family lived Above Ground, in one of the abandoned houses of the dead. All those years ago, after The Flash, Luke recalled using his car, which had mercifully survived that dreadful day and some weeks later, still started. As people were starting to regroup, to re-emerge from wherever they had taken refuge from what had happened, he had driven with the injured Poppy Maitland, to Cornwall. He had helped Poppy to be reunited with her mother, Diana, after which, Luke had wondered what to do. Poppy's gratitude at his gesture of goodwill had not extended to her reciprocating his kindness with an invitation to stay with her and her mother. Luke, coming to realise how far short of his expectations humans actually fell, was not disappointed, merely tired, broken and dispirited. After sleeping in his car for two nights, he realised that there were plenty of houses occupied by dead people and as his need was greater than theirs, so a pretty, three bedroomed detached cottage had become his home after he had buried the family who used to live there.

The house, with its red roof tiles and redbrick frontage had a porch, two living rooms on either side of a narrow hallway at the front, a kitchen and a dining room at the back. Upstairs were two large bedrooms and a smaller room that had belonged to the toddler, the boy whose body was the last one Luke had buried in the field which lay adjacent to the house. Inside was less pleasing that the outside, where a fetid wind had blown the grey ash which was descending from what was once heaven. The interior of the house was thickly blanketed in the stuff and Luke picked his way through it carefully, tears forming in his tired, young face at the sight of the detritus left behind by the family for whom The Flash had meant an instant death. A newspaper on the kitchen table, a radio fallen on the floor. Upstairs, the cupboards in the large, spare bedroom were stripped bare. Luke pondered if the family had intended to leave, or whether the house had been raided by looters, rioters from further afield, looking for whatever they could find to replace what they had lost.

No matter, Luke had thought, the house was his now. He knew that he would have to defend it against anybody whom he didn't want there, namely anyone else like himself, a thief, a marauder. He had been sent, once, on a survival training course – his dad had bought him a weekend 'prepping' experience as a joke birthday present for his twenty-first. There was a sad irony in the fact that what had been a joke between father and son, years ago, was now something which would potentially save Luke's life in the aftermath of the very circumstances his father had tried to prevent.

Shaking his head, Luke had tossed the memory aside. He could not afford to be emotional. He had to protect himself. Chicken wire nailed across the windows, the shutters on the inside of the house, thankfully in working order, locked, would prevent an unwelcome visitor smashing the window and gaining entry. A heavy bookcase against the kitchen door, which was flimsy, old and wooden. He narrowed the entrance hall by piling odd bits of furniture in it. He searched the house top to bottom to find whatever he could use as a weapon. The old days were gone. This was the new normal.

When, eventually, the New Normal Councils were created by those who had sought to reap the benefits gained from the reshaping of society, Luke had had to register his existence to some hefty looking, aggressive 'foot soldiers of the controllers' who had arrived one day with sticks, batons and attitude, his name and his relationship to the former Prime Minister had ensured Luke was registered as an Elite – a person entitled by the grace and generosity of their Leader to remain Above Ground and live his life as a relatively free man.

Free, of course, Luke thought now, being a misnomer if ever there was one. No-one would ever be free again.

'Luke! You are daydreaming again!' Caro's voice broke into

his ruminations and he startled, guiltily.

'It's December the twenty-fourth,' he said, by way of explanation. 'I was thinking about Christmas. Today is Christmas Eve. Do you remember, Caro? I know you're a lot younger than me, but you must be able to remember something. The carols, maybe? The excitement of hanging up a stocking on the fireplace, so that Santa Claus could fill it with presents and surprises, perhaps? Do you remember Christmas dinners? The turkey, the wine, the pudding. How long ago it all seems.'

'I am not interested, Luke, I said, please come and see Zen,' she paused. 'He's coughing. I'm scared.'

All thoughts of the cold, and Christmas and the past faded in those four words – "He's coughing. I'm scared" - as Luke remembered that he used to be a doctor. Caro rushed back up the stairs, with Luke following her as fast as his broken body would allow. He could hear his son's cough even before he reached the small bedroom which used to belong to a dead baby. A dry persistent cough, which accompanied the boy's fever, Luke thought, upon entering the bedroom and seeing his son's flushed face, the beads of sweat under his dark circled eyes.

'How long has he been like this, Caro?' Luke asked, angry that he could live, eat, sleep, breathe with his son and not have known that the child was ill.

'He has been a little tired for a few days,' Caro replied, her anxiety hovering at her son's bedside. 'A little listless, perhaps. The cough is new, Luke, it only started this morning. I shall make the arrangements and report it.'

Luke stopped his examination of his son and stared at his wife – or his "helpmate," as females wedded to older men were called nowadays.

'Report it? What the fuck do you mean, report it? He's your son! He's *our* son, for fucks sake!' Luke kept his voice low, kissed the child's forehead, then grabbed Caro by her forearm and manhandled her roughly out of the bedroom. 'You do realise that they will take him – take us, to a quarantine camp?'

'If it is the virus, then this is where we must be, surely?'

Caro's calm indifference, her blatant and blind support of the New Normal World Order made Luke quail. He felt physically sick. And afraid. He felt very afraid.

'This *"we"* that you speak of, Caro, *"we"* will not do anything. *"We"* will take care of our son, and make sure our other child remains free of the virus. *"We"* will not tell anyone, do you hear? Anyone.' The last word was roared into her face, and Luke had a strange pleasure in seeing her so frightened by the forcefulness he discovered he still possessed. Maybe he had just been waiting for something to matter enough to him again, after everything that did matter, before, had been destroyed.

'Keep Caia separate from Zen,' Luke instructed, speaking more quietly now, but still, his voice carried a menacing tone. 'You and she will sleep in our room. I will sleep with Zen. I was a doctor. Hell, for fuck's sake, I am *still* a doctor. I will tend him. You will look after Caia.' He walked up to his helpmate, his face only inches from hers. 'You will not tell anyone of this. You will not leave the house or speak to anyone. I do not intend for him – or us, to be taken to any quarantine camp. I have seen these camps, I know of them, I know of the conditions, the appalling conditions, in which hostages are kept, and don't tell me those sick and dying people are not hostages, Caro, because we both know that they are. I also know that the survival rate of these quarantine camps is almost zero. So, we will remain here, and I will look after Zen; you will look after Caia.'

Caro pushed him away and tried to move towards the stairs. 'And if I don't?' she asked.

Luke's eyes bore into hers with a determination and ferocity Caro had never known he possessed.

'Then,' he said, very simply, 'I will kill you. Merry Christmas.'

A short story taken from one of Jane Murray's future releases – Resurrection – which is Book Three of the New Normal trilogy, written as Dexter C Channing.

Not in service

By Dawn Treacher

A swathe of fog swirled around the bus shelter, smudging the houses that huddled against the November chill. I fumbled for my ticket that was wedged somewhere in my back pocket between my phone and a packet of chewing gum. My bus was already fifteen minutes late and the thought of walking the two miles home had done nothing to improve my mood. The check out had been tediously busy all afternoon, anyone would have thought they were bringing in food rationing. The headache that had plagued me since lunchtime now felt like someone was playing the bongo drums inside my head.

Out of the fog came the familiar shape of the double decker though the fog was so thick I couldn't read the destination board. What other bus could it be on Otlington High Street? This part of the town wasn't exactly well served with buses. It had long since grown dark, so I frantically waved the light on my phone. I was more than relieved when the bus pulled up to the stop and opened its doors. There was something about the driver that seemed familiar. He reminded me of my granddad, in his profile. I smiled, remembering the man who had been more of a dad to me than my real dad. But the driver dismissed my proffered ticket and nodded with his head for me to sit down. The doors shut, the bus already on its way, rather faster than I had anticipated. I flung myself down in the nearest seat and it was only then that I realised I was the only passenger on board which was odd for a Wednesday.

I cleaned the window with my hand and looked out. Shadows hugged the pavement, the fog now shrouding them like a heavy blanket. I was sure the bus should have stopped again by now, but it was hurtling through the darkness. I couldn't make out the streets of houses nor the parade of shops. I couldn't even see their lights and if I hadn't been imagining it, the bus felt like it was climbing up a steep hill, though there were no hills in Otlington. In fact, I was more and more convinced I wasn't on the right bus at all.

I hung onto the back of the seat in front of me, pulled myself up and edged my way towards the driver but the steeper the bus climbed, the harder it was to hang on. With horror I realised the bus wasn't climbing because it wasn't on the ground at all. Peering out of the window I could see we were travelling above the fog now. Headlights of cars were snaking their way through the darkness below.

We were flying, flying in a bus! I wanted to scream but my voice was in hiding and my heart threatened to explode, it was beating so fast.

"Do sit down," called out the driver.

"But we're...where are we...?" Even trying to force my words wasn't making them flow.

"We're heading for Not in Service, and we won't be there for a while yet."

Not in service? What was he talking about? "I thought you were heading for the Manor Road in Hinchley."

"Then why did you flag me down? It clearly says Not in Service on the front of this bus. Can't you read?"

"Of course...what.... but we're flying...."

The driver leaned his head out into the aisle to look at me. "We have to fly, how else do you expect us to get there?"

I didn't have an answer for that, how could I? I wasn't asleep or drunk, though I wished I was, and I was pretty certain I wasn't dead. We were a long way up, so, either I was going crazy or we really were flying and who had ever heard of a place called Not in Service?

I pulled my phone out of my pocket.

"Don't even bother," called the driver. "There ain't no service up here, not where we're going."

"But where are we going?" My brain just couldn't compute any of this. Why should it? It was weird, no, it was more than weird and if I hadn't been on a bus heading to Not in Service I wouldn't have believed it either.

"Are you visiting anyone in particular?" said the bus driver.

It was then that the horrific thought first occurred to me, maybe this wasn't a bus driver after all, but some deranged serial killer, some futuristic psychopath. He clearly wasn't talking any sense.

"No!" I shouted. "I'm not visiting anyone because no one lives up in the sky, do they? I'm trying to get home, back to my miserable ready meal, to watch some mindless drivel on the telly before going to bed. Only now, you've kidnapped me."

"I haven't done any such thing. How dare you say that."

The bus driver leaned even further into the aisle of the bus, his neat grey hair parted in the middle, his face just like all the other bus drivers, no piercing eyes or strange facial scars. In fact, he looked kind and sweet, like my granddad.

"Why stop my bus if you aren't visiting anyone?"

Okay, so, he may look normal, but he wasn't sounding like it. How could I possibly be visiting anyone up there, wherever that was. If we went any higher, we could be struck by a plane minding its own business on the way back from the Costa del Sol.

"Well, you'd better decide who you want to see before we arrive. I have a tight schedule to meet, and I can't be late back."

Falling back into my seat I peered out of the window. I couldn't jump out, that much was clear and I couldn't make the driver crash either; wasn't that what they suggested you tried to do when locked in a car with a psychopath? So, instead, I decided to engage my potential killer in conversation.

"Who do people usually visit?" I asked, trying unsuccessfully to keep calm.

"To be honest, we don't get many passengers on this route. Those we do get tend not to want to say. Well, it's rather personal, isn't it? Private, you know."

But I didn't know, did I? I had absolutely no idea what he was talking about. I checked my mobile phone and sure enough I had no service.

"We'll be there in five minutes, and I can only stop for twenty. If you don't mind, I'll pay a little visit myself today, it's been a while since I was on this run, and my Mabel would love to have a chat."

His Mabel? Mabel who? How could she be up here, it looked completely empty. Of course, I thought those words too soon because a tiny silver pathway appeared in front of us, not unlike guiding lights on a landing strip and we were heading straight for it. A large dark mass of cloud hung above it and we were speeding so fast I was sure we were about to crash. A brilliant silver light swallowed us up. I closed my eyes and held my breath.

When I opened them again, we weren't in the sky at all, and it wasn't dark either. In fact, it wasn't even November. We were driving through a sweeping park, under a spring blue sky dotted with scudding white clouds. The bus drove along a road that weaved through an avenue of flowering trees. Beside the road stood a bus stop and at the stop was a bench. A woman sat at one end, her white hair piled up upon her head, a rosy glow in her cheeks as if she had just walked a long way. She waved as the bus came to a stop.

"Best think of someone, it gives them a chance to get to the bus stop in time. Mabel's as beautiful as the day I married her. If you'll excuse me," said the bus driver. "I'll be back soon. Mabel loves to walk around the lake."

At this point I should have been relieved that I wasn't going to die but instead I was just so astounded at what I was seeing that I felt as though my brain had gone all soggy.

"Mabel...is she your wife?"

The bus driver turned as he stepped off the bus. "She was, for fifty years and I couldn't manage alone without her if I didn't get to walk around the lake every once in a while."

"But...is she...you know..."

"Dead? Of course she's dead, what's why we're here. Why are you here?"

"Because I thought it was the 640 bus that would take me home."

The bus driver took Mabel's hand and walked away from me. Turning back, he smiled. "I'm ever so sorry, I never thought to check. It would be a shame to miss the chance; there must be someone you'd like to see?"

Then the driver waved his hand, and he and Mabel headed across the park. I watched them walking hand in hand and that's when the thought of Granddad popped into my head. I'd cried so much last summer when he'd slipped away rather too suddenly and unannounced.

I sat down on the bench. The air was warm on my face and cherry blossom wafted on the breeze.

"Fancy seeing you here?"

I turned to see Granddad sitting next to me, the same gentle face and big grin that I always loved.

"I caught the wrong bus," I said which, of course, was true but was so very inadequate.

Granddad just laughed. "Well, I'm very glad you did."

Dawn Treacher has three novels currently published by Provoco, The Seeds of Murder, A Deadly Plot and The

Ninth Life of Norris. All can be found at Amazon and in selected retailers worldwide. Dawn's MG children's books are published by Tiny Tree Publishing.

What did she say?

(A mystery in one brief act).

By A.H. Martin

When this sorry tale kicked off, my wife Cait and I were in the Caribbean for Christmas, with Cait's sister Tina and David, her husband, staying with them at their villa on St Lucia. It was a large, rambling villa, overlooking the golden sands and azure water of a lagoon, fringed by the white waves breaking over the protective reef. Years ago, my wife had deemed it a far more suitable venue to celebrate the holiday season than our much smaller cottage in the Sussex Weald, and we made the trip every year. A hardship I gladly suffered in order to keep her happy.

The two sisters are fraternal twins, not identical, but genetics will out. They have often been mistaken for each other, as they prefer similar hairstyles and clothing. This was never an issue for me, as their differences were apparent. Cait is a fraction taller and has a more willowy body than her sister's voluptuous curves. Tina is the more adventurous of the sisters, Cait's stories of the situations her sister managed to get into as a student were legend.

I was surprised when I first met her husband, as he's a few years older than her. David is something big in the city, exactly what I've never fully understood. He seems to have the Midas touch and was never short of a penny. He's a bit of a cold fish, while Tina is the complete opposite, frivolous and flighty. She is an artist, but unfortunately, she is too lazy to reach her full potential. For every painting she finished, there had to be another ten languishing against the walls of her studio, never to be completed.

Cait is a decent artist, but her artistic skill evolved into an infallible ability to spot art trends and emerging artists and get ahead of the curve. She owns an art gallery featuring modern artists and helps run an art collective. Her original gallery was a tiny shop in the back alleys of Brighton. We met because she needed to expand into a larger space, and I had just what she needed on the ground floor of an old brewery warehouse belonging to my family. I acquired a wife, who got the perfect gallery with her own studio. And an additional studio space to host the art collective of which she was a member.

And then there is me, Michael Lawrence. My family had been medieval grain merchants in the South of England, who took up brewing beer and ales in the seventeenth century. Later, when French brandy, port and sherry became popular in English society, the family began importing (and occasionally smuggling) fine wines and spirits.

Twenty-five years ago, my father bought a farm on the Kent, Sussex border and became a vintner. He planted over ten thousand grape vines on the southern-facing slopes, a mix of Chardonnay, Pinot Noir, and Pinot Grigio.

His goal of making award-winning English champagne was achieved after I took over managing the family's vineyards and winery and hired an oenologist from one of the smaller French wineries. And yes, I've heard all the jokes about British wine.

Now, we make several award-winning wines, one of which is a sparkling wine we can't call Champagne; the French producers would sue our arses off if we did. However, to our credit, we were often ranked in the top ten per cent in blind tastings against popular method champagne brands.

We had been enjoying lunch at the St Lucia Yacht Club with David and Tina, who kept a small yacht moored in the marina. Cait and I knew some of the members, winter visitors like us.

Towards the end of the meal, Tina and David began socialising with other members, wandering off in opposite directions. Cait spotted an artist she knew and went to pigeonhole the woman, eager to display her work at the gallery.

That left me alone at the table. I spotted an old friend who invited me to join him at his table and enjoy an after-lunch drink with him.

His table was on the far side of the terrace, in the shade of a palm tree. The ever-present waiter quickly served us a couple of tall, condensation-covered gin and tonic glasses, heavy on the ice. The cool drink was a pleasure to sip as we exchanged the usual small talk about families and mutual friends.

I was about to ask my friend a question when a hesitant female voice spoke my name from behind me. Glancing over, I saw an attractive blonde-haired, middle-aged woman wearing an expensive dress and shoes. Valuable-looking jewellery hung from her neck and ears. She was sitting with a man at a nearby table.

The woman, who looked familiar, called my name again, and I acknowledged her with a smile, trying to recall her name. She stood, coming over to join us.

"Hi Michael," she said. "I don't know if you remember me; I'm Lucy Thijs, and this is my husband, James." She gestured in the direction of the man sitting at the other table. "We met two years ago at that extraordinary exhibition of Carlo Ribeiro's paintings at your ex-wife's gallery."

Funnily enough, I did recall her; she'd saved me from an excruciating evening. I'd spent an enjoyable couple of hours talking to her and her husband while Cait had been busy dealing with the artist and keeping him away from me. Cait had been his British agent, and she sold many of his paintings. Unfortunately, she had to spend a lot of time dealing with his ego. She'd quickly learned it was best not to discuss anything about the man or his paintings in my presence.

Carlo Ribeiro was everything I'd disliked about an artist and person. Needy, extremely arrogant and demeaning of people outside of the artistic sphere. Believing himself to be the next Salvador Dali, he thinks the world should worship at his feet. Plus, he was a Spanish lech, convinced he was the present-day incarnation of Giacomo Casanova. When Cait first met him, he'd been a gifted artist, but his work had gotten sloppy over the recent years as his reputation and arrogance grew.

As far as I was concerned, his only redeeming feature was that he was now the late Carlo Ribeiro, having died a few months earlier. In my humble opinion, his death in a private plane crash was not a significant loss to the art world, but Cait had been unusually upset.

"How is she holding up?" Lucy asked. "His untimely death must have been such a shock for her."

"It was," I agreed.

Then something Lucy had said earlier finally registered with me. She'd called Cait my ex-wife, yet Cait hadn't mentioned anything about our divorce at breakfast this morning.

I was about to correct Lucy, thinking she must have been mistaken, when she added. "They seemed such a happy couple when I last saw them."

What the hell was going on? "And when was that?" I wanted to know, but I was more than a little confused by the turn in the conversation and concerned by the implications.

Lucy paused to think, "Oh, it must have been four or five months ago. James and I were staying on the Baumgarten's yacht, and Carlo was also there. Cait joined him for a couple of days."

"What, Cait and Carlo were there together?"

She looked puzzled. "Yes, of course. Who else?"

Cait had gone on a trip to Malta around that time; fortunately, her sister Tina had been eager to go with her, as I'd been busy. Cait was there to negotiate a contract with a promising artist she'd heard about. Hoping to host an exhibition of his work later this year. Afterwards, I got the impression from Cait that Tina had been a bit of a handful, and she regretted letting her go with her.

"Where was this?" I'd never heard of the Baumgartens, nor where they lived.

"James and I were spending the summer at our place in Italy, and the Baumgartens have a place nearby. They invited us to spend a few days with them in Malta on their yacht. They were going to celebrate his sixtieth birthday, and as we are old friends of theirs, we were invited to stay with them on board."

"And who are the Baumgartens?" I wanted to know.

"They are Americans. He was the head of a financial institution in New York." Lucy replied. "Rolling in money, she's his second wife, much younger than him." She gave me a confidential look and said in a so-so voice. "At first, I thought she and Carlo were playing around. But then Cait arrived."

I struggled to understand the convoluted conversation but couldn't ignore all the points. The party was in Malta, and Cait and Tina were seemingly there at the same time. She had seen Cait with Carlo and was convinced that Cait and I were now divorced.

"Why would you think that Cait and I are divorced?" I asked, trying to understand.

"Well, you are, aren't you? The Baumgartens told me they were in a relationship, and she was leaving her husband. Because of that, I left them alone, not wanting to embarrass anyone. Oh, I'm sorry if that upsets you."

My mouth was dry; there was a jug of water on the far side of the table, and I stood to pour myself a glass, drinking half in one long swallow. I racked my brains, trying to recall any indication that Cait had been unfaithful, but none came.

"You don't look well; sit back down before you collapse." Lucy pulled my chair out, and I sat down, trying to make sense of everything.

"I'm sorry if bringing up your divorce has upset you." However, she didn't sound that upset.

I shook my head dismissively, "I'm far more surprised to find out that I am divorced. As recently as this morning, I thought I was a happily married man."

"You mean she never discussed a divorce with you. She's been having an affair all this time. How could she do that to you?" Lucy sounded scandalised.

"Sounds like it," I replied bitterly.

"Well, I saw Cait earlier. I'm going to give her a piece of my mind."

She stood up and walked swiftly around the corner of the terrace before I could stop her. I followed; this wasn't something I wanted to be aired in public. I heard voices being raised before I saw them. Lucy was in a deep discussion with a very familiar person who looked shocked and embarrassed. I hurried over. Lucy wasn't the only one who wanted an explanation.

"So, Tina, just what the fuck have you been up to?" I demanded, finally putting two and two together.

A.H. Martin's debut novel, Living Proof is currently available from Amazon and in selected retailers worldwide.

Last Christmas

By Jane Murray

Monty was tired as he lifted the lid up of the bin. A faint smell of rotting rubbish permeated his nostrils, and he wrinkled up his nose in disgust, throwing the scrunched up wrapping paper onto the top of the other waste. He tried to flatten it with his hands but found he didn't really have the energy, and if he was honest, he didn't actually care if the lid of the bin wouldn't shut. So, he wiped his hands on his trousers – he ruefully realised they were his best pair – and he left the bin lid half closed, spilling its gaily coloured, bright, garish wrapping paper out onto the garden. Looking at it with something akin to despair, he shook his head and walked inside.

The kitchen was still untidy. Last night, he'd discovered he didn't have enough room in the dishwasher for all the dirty dishes, but rather than stay up and put the second load in, he'd simply shrugged and gone to bed. He rather regretted the decision this morning. He looked around at what he could see of the worktops. A mixing bowl with a dried-up concoction of – God, what was it in there? He stared into the gloop and couldn't actually decipher what the hell he had made yesterday. Did anyone eat it? Peering into the bowl, he hoped not. There were stacks of dirty plates and dishes, cutlery thrown into the sink, which had been filled with presumably, hot, soapy water but it now had a film of scum on the top of it and, of course, it had gone cold. There was the leftover bird – it should have been covered and put into the fridge, but he'd forgotten. He wondered if the meat would still be edible, fresh? He tried to remember what he'd been taught about cooked meats and failed. Never mind, he wouldn't eat it anyway. He'd find the bin bags and put it in the bin when he had the energy to go out again.

He shuffled into the living room, which was in slightly better shape than the kitchen. At least he had somewhere to sit, he thought, as he shoved a multipack of brightly coloured socks aside, socks that he knew he would never wear. Who had bought them for him? He found the label. Mair had always kept the labels every year, so they would know who had bought for them, so that they would return the favour the next year. Jenny! He smiled. Typical of his youngest daughter, crazy, renegade Jenny. The cleverest of their children, he remembered the disappointment and recrimination when she had dropped out of university in the middle of her second year. Did it matter? Jenny now had her own event management company; she hadn't needed a piece of paper to tell her she could do the job; she'd just gone out and done it! How he loved her. He threw the socks aside. But he didn't love the socks. They would go to the charity shop as soon as it re-opened in the new year.

Settling back into the chair, something dug him in the back and a bit of wiggling and a quite lot of strenuous tugging, he pulled a couple of hangers bearing soft, woollen jumpers. He knew they hadn't been shop bought. They were hand made by Heather, his eldest daughter who made a living and supported her three children without a husband by knitting the most elaborate jumpers and cardigans to order for people rich enough to afford their five-hundred-pound price tag. He would give those back to her, very graciously, but he would tell her to sell them at a knockdown price, get some cash in the bank.

He had been devastated at the loss of Heather's husband, Jerry, five years ago. A tragic accident: Jerry being in the wrong place at the wrong time and an out-of-control vehicle being driven by an old man who'd had a heart attack at the wheel. Both had died instantly and for that, Monty had been thankful. He did not have to sit at Jerry's bedside with his hysterical, terrified daughter, watching machines help him to breathe whilst he held onto the fragile bit of life he still had. He had just – gone and while Heather's grief had been painful for him to experience, he knew Jerry dying quickly and instantly had been a blessing in disguise from God, although if he were honest, Monty didn't quite trust God anymore.

Anyway, less of the morbid thoughts, he chastised himself, sitting more comfortably in his chair now that the hangers and the jumpers had been carefully placed on the sofa. He couldn't believe the prices she was able to charge for a bit of angora wool knitted into a fancy pattern. But that was typical of everything nowadays, he thought, as he reached over to the bottle of 'Glenmorangie' which had been his eldest son's gift to him. He fumbled in the wall unit built into the alcove by the fireplace until he found a glass and then he poured himself a fairly large measure of the spicy, aromatic amber liquid. This was more like it, he thought, as the familiar, warm sensation travelled down his gullet and his stomach contracted with a pain that was almost pleasure.

How long had he been drinking this stuff? Too long, he could hear Mair's voice telling him. It'll be the death of you, she used to say. Well, here he was, still drinking it, still alive, and it had been Mair – tee-total, non-smoking Mair who had gone first. Lung cancer. Stage four. Terminal. And that had been the end of nearly fifty years of marriage. They'd lived nearly that long in this house, he thought, as he stared around the almost neat living room. The fireplace that he'd refused to let Paul, the youngest son knock out when he and his brother David had insisted on 'home improvements' to the house that had seen the births of all four children, the marriages of two and five grandchildren's baptism celebrations. He was glad the fireplace had been saved the worst of the renovations. Where else would his grandchildren have hung their Christmas stockings two nights ago, he thought, taking another gulp of his whisky.

He had enjoyed their excited little faces, the air of frivolity and the sound of the carol singers and the noise of 'Santa's Sleigh' as Tommy from the garage down the road rumbled around the streets, dressed in a red suit and wearing a false beard, sat on the back of the garage's rescue truck, which had been suitably decorated with fake snow, Christmas trees, tinsel and a host of other decorations and oddities that the Highway

Code would have disapproved of. But he collected money and donated it all to charity, so Monty really couldn't see that he was doing any harm. He'd given him a tenner and 'Santa' had got off his 'sleigh' and come right up to the front door to say 'Ho, ho, ho!' and ask the grandkids what they wanted for Christmas.

Getting up to put some more logs on the fire and to give it an enlivening poke, he stood for a moment warming his hands and remembering the days when a fire just like this one had been the only source of heating in the dilapidated, damp old terrace house his family had lived in. Christmas, he recalled, was much simpler then. Dad would go to the woods and chop a small tree down, taking Monty's two elder brothers with him to help him carry it, and the masses of mistletoe and holly boughs they would also return with. Mam would decorate the tree with a few baubles and some tiny little candles; they didn't seem to worry as much about health and safety in those days! Paper chains made by the children, Alfie, Don, Diane, himself and Gracie. They'd sit at the dining table with a pot of glue and some bright coloured paper his mam had bought from the paper shop and Dad would stand on one of the dining chairs and string the chains in loops around the room. The mirror above the fireplace in the parlour would be decorated with the holly and mistletoe would be hung in the kitchen doorway for Mam, hoping to pinch a kiss of Dad while she made the Christmas dinner.

There had been times, he reminisced now, when they'd only been able to afford a tin of potted meat with potatoes, roasted and succulent, and carrots and parsnips from Dad's allotment. The Christmas pudding would be fairly large, and there would be five sixpences in it, one for each of the children. How long Mam and Dad must have saved up to be able to afford to do that. And how different it was now, he thought, as he remembered the crisp twenty-pound notes that Jenny had got from the bank so that he could put one in each of his grandchildren's stockings, hung up on the fireplace.

Thinking of his grandchildren made him think again of his

own childhood, and the camaraderie, sibling rivalry and feeling he always had of being one big family, and a happy one at that, for all its hardship, the poverty, the meanness of Christmas, not in the sense that his mam and dad were tight, but meanness in the sense of how little they'd all had, yet they'd still been happy living in hand-me-downs and playing with second hand toys that Mam had bought from the Salvation Army shop around the corner.

How long ago it all seemed, he sighed, putting down his glass for a moment, while he reached for his medication. He was a bit late taking it today, but it hardly mattered now. Christmas had been wonderful. He fumbled with the foil strips, and popping the brightly coloured pills out of their plastic holders. It should be water that he took his medicines with, but that didn't matter either, he thought, reaching again for the glass.

It had been a good Christmas. Everyone was there, just as Mair liked them to be. One, two, he counted the pills. The smell of the dinner he and Heather had cooked still hung in the air. He should have sprayed some of that cinnamon and apple air fresher, but he supposed it didn't matter now. Three, four. The kids had everything they needed, and they'd all been pleased with the gifts he'd given. The grandchildren loved their grandpop, and they were ecstatic about the twenty-pound notes. It had been money well spent.

He bent down and grabbed a letter out of the unit where he kept his whisky. Best pour another one of those, he thought, as he began to read the letter again.

'Dear Mr. Hardacre,' said the letter. *'Thank you for attending your routine Oncology clinic last week. As you know from your conversation with Mr. Singh, the chemotherapy sessions have now been withdrawn on your instructions as you have opted to cease treatment. We will still call you for regular consultations with your consultant, but this will now be simply a watch and see approach. Please do contact the clinic at any time for any help and advice and there is always the option of hospice care, should you wish to avail yourself of it when you show further signs of deterioration...'*

Five, six. Damn, that whisky tastes good, he thought. Seven. It was getting dark now. Harder to see the little pills. He should have put the light on. He gave a mirthless laugh. As if it mattered.

Eight. Nine. I'm on my way, Mair. Not long now.

What a wonderful last Christmas it had been.

Jane Murray is a multi-genre writer. Her latest novel, written as D.C. Cummings, is a psychological thriller, The Devil's House is available from Amazon and selected retailers worldwide.

Secrets of Scandals Past

By John F. Howard

A small, village parish church in Oxford on a cold, overcast and blustery day was hardly where he wanted to be. The wind bit like the raw emotions of those making their way into the chapel and spilled into the humble surroundings. Guilt, sorrow and anger swirled around the mourners. His death left so many unanswered questions because he'd taken the secrets with him, nestling within his cold, waxen body inside its most expensive coffin. A fitting end to an unfitting death.

Secrets seemed to follow the families and friends around like an unpleasant odour. Whose secrets were they? Were they here today, their owners? Sitting wrapped in their rich, black mourning suits, wearing expressions of sorrow and regret but harbouring a relieved gratitude that their scandal was going to the grave along with the person they were committing to the ground today? Were they really here to grieve, or to protect themselves, these vast numbers of the great and the good, some from the most prominent families in the country. The numbers were many, but the exact figure of those who genuinely cared about the coffin's occupant, far less. This was the society that lived – and died – in the steadfast belief that it was not what you did and how you truly felt, rather how those in your social circle saw and perceived you. Image was, and remained, paramount, and a funeral for one of the members of high society was the perfect occasion to play the role of the sympathetic socialite.

He wondered which camp he fell into. Genuine mourner, or there for the sake of making an appearance? Looking around the small, nineteenth century church building, he found himself wondering why here? Why this tiny backwater church in a village that was a former quarry. Was that a clue to who the deceased had really been? Was nothing real in this life, except for the fact that the man in the coffin had once existed and now he did not, the nozzle of a .38 revolver having been pointed to the side of his head and the pull of the trigger a testimony to a life once lived, ended emphatically by a bullet, and bringing him back to those unanswered questions. But what exactly had driven him to end his life? This was no cry for help or prolonged medical fight to preserve life. The doctors would not be able to save someone whose brains had left their head so brutally, his intentions had been clear and there was no coming back. He had family, opportunity, means and, on the outside at least, a life many envied. Belonging to a family that were one of the first choices on the guest list to every social function of the high society, his life appeared to be a series of social functions, including the most exclusive of soirees and even State banquets. Of course, his social status meant that there had been rumours of affairs, illegal activities, even of being involved in some way with the rising far right political party in Germany, but these had been largely dismissed as idle chit-chat or even a bit of malicious jealousy, as there were many who sought ways to discredit rivals and competitors in less than honourable terms befitting of the British upper class. Prominent, successful people had to endure rivalry and envy, something a number of individuals quite enjoyed, rather than endured, often citing Oscar Wilde's famous line, *The only thing worse than being talked about, is not being talked about.*

No smoke without fire, he thought, bitterly reminiscing of some of the secrets that had caused him so much pain and grief and loss in the winter of 1925. He knew all too well that a secret was only a secret between those who wanted it to remain so or until the accompanying scandal was exposed. Was the pulling of the trigger a coward's way out or the last, final act of ultimate control? A face from the past flashed before him, and he knew the answer to that particular question in Philip Crawford's case. Control. The two dead men were both cut from the same cloth, with the same warped social values. Appearance was everything.

He sighed as the priest began the service. He had been asked to read from the Bible. 'There is a season for everything. A time to live and a time to die,' and he fumbled in the pocket of his greatcoat, making sure he had the papers containing the words he was to read. He was not a man that would have been able to speak from memory. He was not a religious man but then neither was the man in the coffin, whose death had left many devastated, as well as the authorities and the gossip hungry with many unanswered questions, and people wanted answers.

After the service, punctuated by the weeping of those to whom the deceased actually meant something more than a vapid appearance at a funeral, the congregation moved outside for the burial. He watched the expensive, mahogany coffin being lowered into the ground and the chief mourners throwing a handful of earth onto the top of it, obliterating the brass plate bearing the dead man's name, date of birth and date of death. Ashes to ashes, dust to dust. He moved further afield from the gathering, not wishing to see the many emotions being played out at the graveside, some genuine, some perhaps not so well intentioned. It was then he noticed the tall man, disrespectfully clad in a mid-grey tweed coat with dark blue lapels. He tried to remember whether he had seen the man inside the small, cloistered and well attended chapel and thought perhaps this tall man had been seated at the back. Interest piqued, he strode over to the man, who was lighting a long, French cigarette with a Dunhill lighter. Expensive tastes, he thought.

"My condolences."

The tall man's voice was well modulated, with no hint of an accent. Was he just another rich, well-spoken man coming to pay his respects to another rich, well-spoken man, he thought and despised how they all closed ranks, protecting each other, guarding each other's secrets.

His words were contrived and lacked true empathy, but his

opening gambit was polite and had attracted the attention of whom he wanted. He had a smooth, male actor type face, handsome, some would say, but with a predatory look that made him reminiscent of a rodent eagerly eyeballing his next meal. Now with his target in focus, he waited to see what response, if any, he would get. And he wouldn't have to wait long.

"Thank you," came the reply, the speaker experiencing an emotional turmoil that was being hidden behind a carefully constructed look of dignity that his family had been perfecting many years before he was even born. Even in grief, image and social standing would always be paramount. What had Philip Crawford said once, *'You're in high society now, boy,'* and high society had high expectations and low morals.

"Such a shame," the tall man's face tried to portray a look of empathy. "What drives a man with such a respected reputation to end his life via in his own hand?"

"He didn't," said a voice from behind them. "I killed him."

The above excerpt is the Prologue from John's second book in the Crawford Chronicles, available in 2026. John's first book, A Scandal of Secrets, is available now from Amazon and selected retailers.

Scarlett Road

By Dawn Treacher

On fumes, the hatchback coasted to the verge, running over a coke can, already squashed beyond recognition. Cranking open the door, Scarlett let in a squally wind, pin pricks of rain landing on her face. A glance in the wing mirror confirmed what she already knew; that she had stopped on a road that cut across a hill, the trees curved against the wind, fields of frosted grass stiff and tall. The only other occupant she could see a crow digging deep into the carcass of a rabbit.

Grabbing a bag from the seat next to her, Scarlett got out, searching behind her; the horizon smudged by a mist that coated her hair with fine droplets. Slamming shut the door she pulled the bag over her shoulder and headed north, keeping to the tarmac, her slip-on shoes rubbing at the heels of her bare feet.

Her mother would have told her it was stupid to have bare feet until well gone April, but Scarlett had long given up listening to her mother's advice. Her mother had stopped bothering to say anything at all since Scarlett had abandoned going to lectures and no longer returned her mother's calls. The wind found its way through the thin cardigan that Scarlett held tightly around her body, lifting the dark roots of her hair, playing across the bruise that shaded her cheek and made her left eye hard to open.

She left the car behind her, pushing on over the crest of the hill, past a crop of trees that bent away from the wind, a flock of crows buffeted in their branches. Scarlett wasn't cut out for university anyway. She's only gone to escape the suffocating terrace that she shared with her mother, regrets and what ifs clinging to the walls alongside the graduation certificate of her sister, Clarence, who had had the indecency to set up home in Australia with a city lawyer, raising a child her mother could only hope one day to meet. University life for Scarlett had offered colour beyond the beige and cream, excitement out of reach of the cul-de-sac where everyone knew what everyone else was doing and how often they went to the shops. A bunch of curtain twitchers who tutted when Scarlett walked home late, a little unsteady on her feet, her dyed hair as loud as the music that throbbed in her ears.

The road fell away, curving into a valley. A rabbit poked its head out of the grass verge. A wood pigeon perched on a fence post, its feathers fluffed up to the size of a large ball, its eyes closed, swaying slightly in the wind. The trees to her left grew thickly now, their branches intertwined, the wind whistling through them. Scarlett shivered. The cold penetrated the striped t-shirt beneath her cardigan, its neck scooped low. Her hand pulled the edges of her cardigan together, a spray of dried blood across her knuckles, the cuff of her right arm stiff, the blood now a brownish crust.

The sound of a car made her stop. In the distance she could see it emerging out of the mist, heading inevitably towards her. She pushed her way over the grass verge, the wetness of the grass soaking her feet. She threaded through the hedgerow and crouched down in a ditch behind, her breath like smoke, a ripple of goosebumps spreading up her legs, her jeans tight around her thighs as she squatted. Through the twigs of Hawthorne, Scarlett watched a blue estate car drive past, an elderly couple in the front, a dog barking on the back seat, its face squashed up against the window. Then they were gone. Scarlett waited. Nothing. The road was empty again and she sat alone, her only company an insect that crawled through the grass by her left foot and the call of the wood pigeon overhead.

Back on the road, Scarlett walked briskly, her shoulder bag bumping against her thigh as she made her way down the hill. The letter in her back pocket crinkled as she walked. She had read it so many times she knew it by heart. It had arrived, forwarded by her mother, or at least it must have been her mother, as no one else knew where she was staying. Those friends she had met at university had all drifted away, moving into detached houses with neatly tended gardens, well planned pension schemes and three-piece suites. All that is except Suzie, who still texted occasionally, shared a drink in a pub that wasn't too loud but even she had not answered Scarlett's messages in the last couple of months. It suited Malcolm, an exclusivity that meant their evenings were undisturbed, the flat above the takeaway free from gossip and the hassle of hospitality. The only time Suzie had called round, Malcolm had stood in the kitchen, cigarette in his hand, his arm guarding the kettle, daring Scarlett to move it. Suzie's invitation to the pub went unanswered by Scarlett as Malcolm's nicotine-stained fingers drummed the Formica work top, his eyes never leaving Scarlett's. He told Suzie that Scarlett needed an early night, that she had a headache. Though Scarlett found herself nodding in agreement she doubted Suzie believed her. Suzie never called again, not after Malcolm escorted her out, whispering something in her ear as he opened the door. The whisky fumes on his breath walked outside with her. Scarlett had watched her out of the window as Suzie walked down the road, dodging a group of youngsters laughing over their kebabs. When Suzie looked back, Scarlett pulled the curtains closed so she couldn't see her face. She knew what Suzie was thinking but Malcolm loved her, like no one had loved her before. It was just that sometimes she made stupid mistakes. She tried, she really did, only Malcolm didn't accept mistakes, unless, of course, they were his own.

Reaching the bottom of the hill the road levelled out. The mist had lifted letting the pigeon grey sky lighten to a cold blue before her. A couple of miles ahead a village snuggled together to keep warm, a cluster of roofs visible on the horizon. Scarlett kept walking. She touched her back pocket, felt the letter inside. It had arrived a few days ago, when Malcolm had nipped to the shop. When he returned with a loaf of white sliced, two cans of beans, a newspaper and a packet of cigarettes, Scarlett had already hidden it in a pair of shoes shut in a box stuffed at the back of the wardrobe. She wondered if her mother realised who the letter was from and why he had written it. She must have recognised the handwriting, they had after all been married for over fifteen years before he walked out, leaving behind just an old pair of trainers and a stain on the armchair where he usually sat. Her mother never said why he left, though Scarlett hadn't failed to notice the arguments late at night, the times he never came home at all. The day her father left he hadn't said goodbye, there was only an emptiness that her mother had been trying to fill ever since. He had sent a card for her eighteenth birthday and fifty quid but nothing since, until this letter. The letter which tried to explain the silence. Scarlett wanted to believe him, wanted to believe in someone. Her mother's disappointment had made her shrivel inside and Scarlett could only shrink away from it. Malcolm, she had believed in Malcolm. He had made her laugh, driven fast, offered the sort of adventure that her mother had tried to protect her from.

The bruises on her arms still hurt, where Malcolm's fingers had squeezed too tightly, when he shook her. All she had done was share a coffee at lunchtime with the others from work. She hadn't answered his call, why should she, his calls were intrusive, always breaking into her thoughts at lunchtime when she tried to eat her packed lunch, having declined yet again to join the others for a sandwich at the pub.

A truck headed towards her, leaving the village, changing down a gear in readiness for the hill. Scarlett kept walking. She pulled a mobile from her bag, the screen a craze of cracks. No signal. She put it away. Her father had given her a number to call, not a mobile but it wasn't local either. As soon as she had a signal again, she would call it, leave a message. He hadn't forgotten her, just needed time to realise what was important. Scarlett wished she had realised earlier herself, but it was too late for that now. She saw the village sign up ahead, round a bend in the road. A ditch ran alongside her, beyond it a huddle of cows stood in a field, their hooves churning the mud. She reached into her bag again and pulled out a vegetable knife, the blade still wet with blood. A few spots spattered the road, glistening scarlet. She threw it into the ditch where it sank into three inches of water, out of sight. Malcolm hadn't been expecting that but that's where he had underestimated her. She remembered that disbelief in his eyes as she pushed the knife into his chest, as he sank to the floor and didn't get back up again.

Scarlett took a red scarf out of her bag, tied it around her blond hair and pulled her cardigan up to her chin. She headed into the village, leaving the road behind her.

Dawn's three novels, The Seeds of Murder, A Deadly Plot and The Ninth Life of Norris are all available with Provoco Publishing, via Amazon or selected bookstores. Dawn's fourth novel, a psychological thriller, will be available in early 2026.

Finding Jack

By Ella Blackthorn

We all know the routine. Romance flourishes in the beginning with sparkling hearts and expressions of affection. The thrill of the chase, romantic dinners by candlelight and door openings, before it all settles down to farting in front of the TV wearing boxer shorts. Not to mention the leisurely breakfasts in bed that disappear as quickly as the waistline you had in your twenties.

However, from the get-go, Jack had been as romantic as a doorknob. So, on an otherwise uneventful Valentine's Day morning, Caroline had got herself ready for work alone as her unromantic beloved was working away from home. After dressing in her pale blue trouser suit, she manoeuvred her long, light blonde hair up into a bun and applied a light amount of makeup. She never wore it outside of work as she liked the fresh peach and cream of her complexion. Therefore, she compromised by wearing a little mascara and lipstick when she went to the office or court.

After a swift breakfast, she was putting her files she'd worked on last night into her bag when there was an unexpected knock at the door. She frowned. It was far too early for the postman. She opened the front door, and there on the doorstep of their terraced house was a massive bouquet of flowers, but looking up and down the street, she couldn't see a van or a soul in sight.

'Weird,' she said to herself, taking the delivery into the house.

They'd agreed to do 'Valentine's Day' when he was next home, so had he suddenly had an unexpected surge of romance and sent her a surprise?

Jack worked in IT for a firm in London, where he stayed half the week and came home on Thursday nights. If he'd been

133

home at that moment, he would have got very lucky indeed. However, she was home alone and had no one to throw her down wildly on the sofa.

She carried the stunning velvety red roses into the kitchen and laid them on the granite island top. Half in excitement, the other wondering what had got into her boyfriend of eighteen months. She carefully opened the envelope in anticipation. On one side, there was a picture of red and white roses and Happy Valentine's in red typescript, on the other just a sequence of dots and dashes.

-.. .- -. --. . .-. --..-- .-.. . .- ...- . -. --- .——

At first, she stared at the card, feeling bemused, but then a warmth spread through her. The flowers were fragrant and so beautiful, and they must have cost him a small fortune. She looked at the card again, thinking it must be some joke from Jack that he wanted her to decipher, knowing how she enjoyed a good TV detective story. However, she couldn't make head or tail of it. What was Jack up to? Had he suddenly got the romance gene? She loved romance, and in the beginning, it was apparent that Jack hadn't a clue, so in a way, she settled for the no bumps in the road type of relationship. He was honest, reliable, and thoughtful, but what drew Caroline to him was that he came baggage-free and without drama.

She knew that he was never normally reachable by phone during the day. They had to leave all personal belongings in lockers when they got in the building he'd told her, so she knew it was unlikely he'd answer if she rang. On a day-to-day basis, any emergencies had to wait until after seven when he got back to his hotel. Like the day the water tank exploded in the loft, sending water cascading through the ceiling and light fittings, and soaking the landing carpet. Caroline was resourceful though; she'd looked after herself quite nicely for nearly 20 years of her life before meeting him. By the time he'd returned home, the tank had been replaced, the ceiling was repaired, and there was a new carpet up the stairs and landing. Not that he noticed.

So, putting the flowers in a vase next to the sink to arrange properly later, she sent him a quick text.

'Thank you so much for the lovely flowers, Jack, they're amazing. Happy Valentine's Day darling. Not sure what the message means, but I'm sure I can figure it out after work. Love you lots, C x.'

Realising that she was now running late, she headed out of the door to work at the top of the High Street.

Mistleton was a small town in North Yorkshire that, on the whole, was slow-moving and quiet, except for market days. That was when the sounds of cows and sheep being unloaded could be heard before being sold from the nearby cattle market. Close by, visitors enjoyed people watching with hot lattes and buttered sourdough at the local café on the market square.

Caroline's office overlooked the market on one side and the shops and cafés on the other. She'd qualified as a solicitor in her twenties and joined one of the firms as their family lawyer, dealing primarily with the marital breakdowns of the town. Her cases were mainly infidelity-based or spouses escaping narcissistic endings. The clients ranged from farmers who'd cheated on their wives, shopkeepers who'd run off with a member of staff, or the latest one, the chef at the large hotel who had disappeared with the takings, AND one of the chambermaids. There was never a dull moment in her job. Over the years, she'd become known to many upset exes when things went wrong, as sometimes they did. In others, she was the best thing since sliced avocado on toast when she'd surpassed their often-rigorous needs.

She liked her job, but the constant arguments and bills that increased when clients disagreed out of spite took their toll on some weeks. This was where her real passion came into play. She adored painting and, in recent years, had sold quite a few and had her first exhibition at the local gallery last summer. It had got to the point now where she felt that she was working to fund her paint addiction. The coming weekend, she and Jack were heading to the Lakes so he could read, and she could paint and do the belated romance, so receiving the flowers had been an added surprise.

'Was he gearing up to propose?' she thought.

Being a usual Tuesday, it was market day, and the hustle and bustle of her diary meant that she barely had time to grab a sandwich from the local deli before she had back-to-back appointments for the rest of the afternoon. She noticed that Jack had read her text, which was unusual since he didn't normally do so, but he hadn't replied, which was even more unusual. She knew his job was full on, although they never really talked about his work. Computers and IT at his level were beyond her. Sometimes he would tell her something about coding, but the blank expression on her face would make him stop. Since her work was confidential, they didn't tend to discuss what she did either. She'd never met his colleagues as she hated the craziness of London, and he didn't often meet hers as he didn't like parties. Her friends thought it was weird, but it suited them both.

She'd often daydreamed about a surprise proposal, Jack going down on one knee and sweeping her off her feet just like in a corny Hollywood movie, but he was more likely to do it over a bacon sandwich on a Sunday morning whilst reading the papers. Perhaps he would do it when they were away? He'd planned the whole holiday, which wasn't like him. Usually, she booked and planned it all.

The day dragged on, and Jack still hadn't replied. Her four o'clock appointment had been cancelled, so she decided to go home early. Just as she was preparing some files to take home with her, she was buzzed by her secretary.

'Could she see a walk in before she left for the evening?'

Caroline sighed. She wanted to get home, admire her roses again, and hopefully catch up with Jack when he got home. But instead, she agreed, and within a minute, a tall woman with raven black long hair entered the room. Despite being around six feet in height, she wore red spiked heeled shoes, sheer tights, and a fitted black knee-length dress.

Mistleton liked to think of itself as gentrified with its posh bread and cafes with large umbrellas, but this woman looked like she'd stepped out of the pages of Vogue. She didn't exactly fit in with the town and its market square, with the pungent smell of cow dung and straw blowing around the paths.

Trying to hide her surprise, Caroline indicated the empty chair on the other side of her desk, and they both sat.

'How can I help you... Mrs. ....?' she paused, realising her secretary hadn't given a name.

'Mrs. Jones, Jane Jones,' she responded. Caroline noticed the perfectly applied makeup, dark, almost black eyes, and unlike most of her clients, there wasn't a tear-stained cheek in sight.

'What can I do for you, Mrs. Jones, or shall I call you Jane?'

'Mrs. Jones is perfectly acceptable,' she replied with an accent Caroline couldn't place at all. It was not from Yorkshire. She sounded very refined, as though her accent had been ironed out of any hint of commonness or geography. 'I want to divorce my husband right now, and with as little fuss as possible.'

'I'm sorry to hear that. How long have you been married,' Caroline asked, starting to write on her yellow notepad.

'Twelve years, we haven't had any children, we own some houses,' she replied briskly. 'We both worked in the city, but he retired, and I've inherited my parents' estate. Can I get out of the marriage and still keep what's mine?'

Caroline frowned. 'Did you have a prenup when you married?'

'No prenup. He had more than I when we married, and he didn't want one. I haven't told him I want a divorce. Can you do that?'

'Well, that's not normally how it's done. Wouldn't it be best to have a conversation? Do you want someone else to tell him because you're afraid he'll hurt you?'

Her client stood up abruptly.

'This isn't going to work. Thank you for your time.'

And before Caroline could utter a word, Mrs. Jones had left her office and by the slam of the front door shortly after, she'd left the building too.

There was a knock at the door, and her secretary Julie came in.

'That was odd. Is she ok?'

'I've no idea at all. I asked the usual questions, and she got up and left. I very much doubt she's called Mrs. Jones!'

Julie nodded. 'Maybe she'll be back?'

'Maybe. Well, I'll get off now. I'm in court first thing tomorrow, then have the afternoon off, so I won't see you until Thursday.'

'Yes, it's in my diary. Have you got the files you need?'

Caroline nodded, said her goodbyes, and walked back home. Despite it being February, the weather had been kind, and although cold, the blue sky at lunchtime had been refreshing; now, however, it was almost dark as she trod the familiar paths home.

As she crossed the road towards her front door, she saw that the front room light was on; she frowned. Had Jack come home early?

Eagerly, she unlocked the door and called out 'Jack' as she closed the door behind her.

The house was silent; the lights were on in both the front room and kitchen. Had she forgotten to turn them off? It was then that she felt a cool breeze, and she saw that the back door was open, with glass scattered across the terracotta-tiled floor. Anxiously looking over to the sink, she saw that her beautiful flowers were strewn on the floor, the vase on the worktop still full of water, and the card which she'd left next to it was gone. Going back down the hall, she glanced into the front room and saw that the cushions were thrown on the floor, and the rug was askew.

'Oh God, what if the intruder was still in the house?' she thought.

Fear rose within her as she moved swiftly out into the street, dialling 999 as she closed the door behind her. The responder assured her that help was on the way as she unlocked her car and sat and waited inside. Her neighbouring houses were all Airbnb rentals, so she knew there was no one else she knew to help nearby. A short time later, the police arrived and conducted a quick search of the house, but no one was inside. The back door had been forced, so a locksmith came and repaired it in super-fast time. That was the thing about living in a small town: you could always find a tradesperson.

On closer inspection, nothing had been taken other than the card, and the police questioned her as to whether she had perhaps just misplaced it. They suggested that it must have been mischievous kids who'd broken in as a joke if they knew the house was empty. Caroline admitted she was a creature of habit, leaving the house at the same time each day and getting home just after five. Maybe they were right. He suggested that she use the house alarm in the future, something she rarely did. It was a quiet, safe town, and she'd only set it when she went away with Jack.

After they'd all left, Caroline retrieved the flowers and put them back into the vase, hoping that they wouldn't die through a day on the cold tiled floor. She felt shaken up that someone had broken in and been in their house. She checked all the doors and windows again and had just sat down with a cup of tea when she realised it was almost seven and time to call Jack as she always did when he was away. Usually, it rang a few times before he answered but today was different. It instantly kicked in with a message.

'The number you have dialled has not been recognised, please check the number and try again.'

Looking down at her mobile, she dialled the preprogrammed number again and got the same message instantly.

'What the hell,' she exclaimed, then googled the name of the hotel he always stayed in when he was away. Finding it, she dialled the number.

It was answered by a woman with a very South London accent. 'The Charlton Hotel, how can I assist you?'

'Can you put me through to Jack Hunter please, tell him it's Caroline Hirst.'

After a short pause, the receptionist came back onto the line. 'I'm sorry, but we don't have anyone by that name staying here madam.'

'Please could you look again; he always stays at your hotel.'

'I'm sorry madam, there's no guest here of that name, or on our system. Is there anything else I can help you with?'

Caroline was dumbfounded and garbled, 'No' to the receptionist, who hung up the phone.

She tried his mobile one more time, but the same message was repeated over and over again.

Staring down at her phone, she felt paralysed with fear and confusion, her hands shaking, her breath catching in the back of her throat.

'Where was Jack? What was going on?'

Ella Blackthorn joined Provoco in 2025, after having self-published a number of novels. Her debut for Provoco, Finding Jack, is due for release in 2026.

Silent Night

By Jane Murray

Roxanne sighed and relaxed her shoulders. Everything had gone according to plan. She'd not relished the thought of holding a Boxing Day for James' friends and colleagues from work, but it had all gone according to plan, and she had managed to get through it. She quickly walked around the large lounge, which had been beautifully and artfully decorated for the Christmas festivities, and collected the empty, dirty wine and champagne glasses, placing them on a large, wooden tray which she and James had bought on one of their many holidays abroad. She recalled the tray had been bought in Marrakesh and remembered the circumstances when she'd realised the cost had far exceeded the budget James had set for purchases. Sighing, she went into the kitchen and shuddered both at the mess and the memories.

She focussed on the mess, because she couldn't do anything about the memories.

Working methodically around the kitchen, the wine and champagne glasses she handwashed, they were too delicate for the dishwasher. She plunged them into warm, soapy water to let them soak while she walked around the large central island, putting things away, clearing condiments, putting spices back on the rack, collecting leftovers and placing them on a large serving platter which she covered with tin foil and put in the fridge. Then, she gathered all the dirty dishes, rinsed them and stacked them in the dishwasher. She was so tired, she thought she could fall asleep standing up. The last plate had just been put into the bottom rack in the machine, and Roxanne was straightening up, rubbing a weary hand over a tired face, when her husband walked in.

Considering how late it was, James looked remarkably bright in comparison to his wife who was almost drooping with tiredness. He gave her a look and glanced around the kitchen, noting that the countertops hadn't been washed down and there was still a sink full of washing up to be done.

'Is the dishwasher broken, Roxie?' he asked, raising his eyebrows.

'No, James. It's the glassware. I don't put those in the dishwasher. They're fine, they're soaking and I'll leave them to drain while I clean the countertops and the floor.'

'The cloakroom needs tidying,' was all he said before he selected a clean glass and a fresh bottle of red wine from the rack by the door.

Roxanne watched him in dismay. How long was he going to sit up, drinking wine? She needed to go to bed.

'Err, James…' she began and he turned, giving her a questioning look. The eyebrows raised again.

'Yes, Roxie?'

'Oh… nothing. Never mind. It can wait.' Like she would be, she thought, resentfully as he took the wine and his glass through the double doors that led from the kitchen into the morning room. Why was he sitting in there, she thought. He was such a stickler that the room only be used for breakfast, and only up until eleven in the morning, after that, brunch would be served in the dining room or people would move through to relax after breakfast in the lounge. She gave him a resentful glance as he settled himself down on one of the armchairs artfully arranged in front of the floor to ceiling brick fireplace. Why sit there, when the fire wasn't lit? Then, the answer came to him as their eyes met.

'Slacking, Roxie?' he eased the cork out of the bottle and began to pour the wine. The glug – glug – glug annoyed Roxanne, reminding her of good times that she didn't have any more, and of the indulgence and entitlement James coveted.

She shook her head silently, not daring to answer and turned her back on him as he laughed quietly to himself, but not quietly enough that she couldn't hear his mirth. A feeling she couldn't decipher welled up inside her as Roxanne headed for the cupboard where the mop was kept.

'Don't forget about those glasses will you, Roxie?' James called.

Feeling her shoulders rise with tension, Roxanne took several deep breaths and tried to calm down. She hated being called Roxie. Her name was actually Persian, derived from the Persian word 'Roshan' which meant 'light' or 'radiance' because she was born at dawn, but her mother didn't like the name Dawn. Why did he always have to make everything about her feel common? Roxie sounded like a dog's name!

He hadn't always been like this, so tense, so wound up, so critical of her, Roxanne thought, as she found the special waxes and oils she needed to clean and protect the wooden worktops and butcher's block. She was so tired; all she wanted to do was go to bed. Strip off her nice outfit that she'd picked especially for Boxing Day, throw it in the laundry basket and put on her comfy, old pyjamas and bed-socks then get into bed and sleep as late as she could get away with.

Wiping down the butcher's block, she heard James' voice again.

'Glasses, Roxie!'

'Yes, I know!' she snapped back, and then immediately realised her mistake. James did not like being talked back to.

He rose from his armchair and strode into the kitchen, glancing with displeasure at the still untidy kitchen. He took in the mop, propped up against one of the countertops, the bottle of floor cleaner next to it. The bottles and tins of oil and wax were scattered across the big island in the middle of the kitchen, a quarter of which was a custom-built butcher's block, which Roxanne was currently in the middle of waxing. There were used cloths and rags heaped untidily next to blender. In the huge stainless-steel sink, the precious crystal glassware was still in soak. Bubbles rose from the sink, looking like a huge, uneven mountain range covered in snow.

James had switched on the radio in the morning room and the sounds of a recording of 'Carol's from Kings' was playing in the background, drifting into the kitchen mingling with the tension and displeasure.

Roxanne recognised 'Good King Wencelas' and thought how beautiful the male voices sounded. Some of them were still little boys with voices that hadn't yet broken. They were still innocent, not grown yet into men that were full of anger, who created an uneasy atmosphere when they were standing behind you.

'What's all this, Roxie? Are you growing a backbone? Answering back. Tut, tut. That won't do at all, will it?'

It was intimidating, having James watch her every move, and the menace in his voice frightened her. She heard her mother's voice in a small recess at the back of her mind, which was whirling in fear and trepidation.

'I don't like him, Roxanne,' said her mother's long dead voice. 'He gives me the creeps, and I don't like the way you kow-tow to him and hang on his every word. You can always come home to me and Papa, you know.'

She remembered what she said to her mother at the time, 'But he loves me, Mother. You'll grow to like him.'

But Roxanne's mother did not grow to like her son-in-law and over the years, her suspicion about his treatment of her daughter grew as Roxanne's personality seemed to diminish. And then Brenda Collins got ill and passed away before she could air her misgivings to anyone, before she could conjecture about the bruise on her cheekbone; the sprained wrist; the bruises on her upper arm. Brenda Collins was unable to tell anyone, and Roxanne took to wearing high neck blouses and long sleeves. Heavier make up helped to cover up any marks on her face.

James smiled unpleasantly at his trembling wife. He liked it when he knew he had riled her and that she was powerless to resist him. If she fought back, he hit harder and eventually, she stopped fighting.

'I'm sorry,' Roxanne said to him now. 'It's just that it's late, and I'm so tired – it's been a long day.'

'There you go, again, Roxie. I really am going to have to teach you to be more grateful.'

His hand moved so fast that she didn't even see it as it struck her face. Her head flashed to the side, and she raised her own hands to fend off any further blows.

'It's been such a good Christmas, Roxie, darling. Why on earth are you spoiling it with your incessant moaning?' he sneered, and turned his back, walking towards the morning room again as Roxanne, straightening up, caught a glimpse of the butcher's block and the knife drawer.

Finally enraged at his treatment, his ingratitude, his cruelty, she swiftly drew one of the large meat knives out of the drawer and ran at him, calling his name.

She plunged the knife into his chest as he turned around and she had the pleasure of seeing sheer terror in his eyes, as he realised what she had done. She could have told him about the terror, and what she felt every single day whilst she lived on tenterhooks, not knowing whether she had done anything wrong or whether he would simply want to take his bad mood out on her already battered body.

He put his hands up to his chest as she drew the knife out and she watched as the blood flowed out of the small incision the knife had made. Such a small cut, she thought, and so much blood. She smiled with satisfaction and with a strength she did not know she possessed, she plunged the knife into him a second time. This time he fell to his knees as he made a gurgling sound which she thought sounded like 'Help me,' but she couldn't be sure.

'I can't hear you, James,' she said. 'Let me go into the morning room and turn off the radio.'

She left the knife in his dying body, left the blood to gush out of the two wounds she had made, left James to fall forward as his soul left his body and went to wherever would let him in for eternity.

She stood in the morning room and stopped to simply stand and listen to the carol being sung. Such a sweet voice ringing out, soaring into the cloisters in the university cathedral. The same university she had once attended before she met James.

'Silent night, holy night…' sang the choirboy on the radio and Roxanne smiled, safe in the knowledge that it would be.

Jane Murray's latest novel, written as D.C. Cummings, is a psychological thriller, The Devil's House is available from Amazon and selected retailers worldwide.

The Only Ones Left

By K.E. Jennings

"Oh.... Merry Christmas, baby! Christmas comes this time each year!"

Music rings out in the house, the notes loudly echoing off the walls. The Beach Boys always cheer me up, no matter the season. I set cereal bars out with bottled OJ for breakfast, the easiest thing to 'make'. We begin to eat, but Cole begs me to get out our Christmas decorations so we can have some fun decorating. I want to concede with his wishes but know that we need sustenance.

Dang, it really is almost Christmas, in one week.

"After breakfast, Cole. If you eat everything and drink all your juice, I'll lug everything out. Deal?"

"Deal!" he agrees.

I watch his dark hair bob along to the music as he takes bites of his food. My mind wanders back to the fact someone else is alive, just like us. Or at least it certainly appears that way. I must be sure before I can accept it as fact. And honestly, I'm not sure I'm ready to do that yet. Having another anxiety attack is not appealing, nor sustainable.

Check it. Just flipping check, it.

Darn inner dialog. I desperately want to ignore it, for now, but the voice in my head has a point. How can I know if I don't check? I sit at the end of the dining table, across from Cole, and pick up my phone. There is a message from the stranger.

Hi, my name is Ian. Are you alive? I got a notification stating you'd requested to be friends, but there are no other people here in the entirety of Sydney. Nor anywhere in the country that I can gather. I see you are living in America. Is this correct? It's just past midnight here, but I'm staying awake for a bit to see if you'll message me back. PLEASE do, if you get this!

I sit stunned. He is real, as real as I am. The words leap out from the screen on the phone. This is good news. I've been searching for others for months to no avail. I re-read the message a few dozen times. There isn't *anyone* in Australia? Just him? How stunningly odd. My gut twitches, telling me that he is still familiar, though I can't connect how. But I need to.

I am cautious, not sure if I should write back right away, or wait. Maybe I should at least let him know he isn't alone? The facts hit me hard as I decide what to do. We finally aren't alone!

Ian, I'm Malia. I didn't know anyone else was alive! My son and I are the only ones here. I have a lot of questions but won't overwhelm you right now, and you probably want to sleep. It looks like you are 16 hours ahead of us. Please let me know if you get this.

Hitting send, I stop short of typing everything I want to ask. Short and sweet is best. It all begins to sink in but at the same time feels like a dream.

We aren't alone!

Cole has finished eating and is sitting at the table, staring at me. He has a sweet little grin on his face. I know he wants to decorate the tree. It is his favorite Christmas activity to do.

"Are you ready?" I ask him, returning his grin.

"YES!" he shouts at me with a giggle.

This is just what he needs, and me for that matter. We aren't alone and it is about to be the most magical holiday for a young child. Things are looking *up*.

After much cussing under my breath, I manage to get the tree down from the garage ceiling rack. Twenty feet up is no small feat. I hate heights and ladders. Both are essential though for getting the tree and decoration boxes down. This used to be a Joshua task, but I managed to do it all by myself.

I've got this.

My husband would be so proud.

Cole jumps up and down and runs circles around the living room as I cart the boxed tree in with both arms. Letting it thud on the large area rug; I gingerly stretch my arms which ache with stiffness. I am out of shape! When I used to surf actively, I could carry anything that was heavy with no problem. But now, not so much. Making a mental vow to begin lifting weights again, I bend down and begin working on the metal tree stand. Nothing is better than lights dimmed at night with our sparkling Christmas tree illuminating the space. It is always so peaceful.

Ding!

The phone notifies me from the table. I feel my heart beat a bit faster. Is it from excitement? Nervousness? I think it is both. Being void of all other adult conversations for *so long* has been hard. The toll that it has taken on me is beginning to be evident. Having a good conversation is a wonderful prospect. It also doesn't hurt that the person communicating with me is handsome.

Don't think that way. He could be dangerous for all I know!

Guilt hits me immediately after the thoughts. I might be married but I can still have a normal conversation with a man, right? It won't mean anything. Besides, I need to find out more about what happened to us, how we got left behind. Maybe he has more information. I wrestle the tree together and stand back to look at my handywork.

"All right! Here we go!" I exclaim.

I plug in the Christmas tree lights just as Cole walks over. The lights glow brightly with tiny white and golden yellow hues. It is simply beautiful.

"Mommy! It's so pretty!"

He claps and watches the lights with awe on his face. This is my favorite part, seeing his joy and wonder. Cole is so innocent and easy to please, especially at this time of year.

I clap my hands. "Let's get hot cocoa, do you want some, son?"

He nods at me and reaches for the TV remote. Requesting to watch something with Christmas in it, I help him find a suitable classic. 'Rudolph the Red-Nosed Reindeer'. Once his attention is focused on the movie, I grab my phone and lean against the kitchen counter. With a soft exhale, I tap on the app.

It's not too late here. I'm wide awake. I can't believe you're real! And alive! You said you are there with your son? How old is he?

I see on your profile that you're married. Did your husband disappear? I am engaged but my fiancé isn't here. She was next to me in bed the night it happened. She was pregnant with our child. We never found out if it was a boy or girl, it was too early to tell.

When I woke up the next morning, both were just gone. Everyone is gone. All my neighbors, all my coworkers, every single bloody living mate I've ever known are GONE. Have you been looking for others? I tried for weeks. Drove around everywhere. Nothing!

Sorry if this is overwhelming. I'm rambling. I just wanted to talk. You have no idea how hard it's been to not have anyone to talk to!

His words sound excited to connect to me, to *someone*. And I can't blame him. I feel the same way. Glancing at my son, watching TV, I decided not to tell Ian too much yet, about Cole. No harm in talking about myself. But with Cole, I want to be cautious. I don't even know this guy! Is he *really* in Australia? I type a reply.

I do understand not talking to anyone else. My son is young.

It was the same way for me, went to bed next to my husband and by morning, he was gone. I searched the house and the neighborhood for him but quickly saw that everyone else was gone too! I don't know about you, but it was the single most terrifying day of my entire life.

Do you have any theories as to how this happened? Why it did? I've been going crazy trying to figure it out.

I close the app and begin to make the promised hot chocolate. A feeling of calm slowly begins to settle into the cracks of my mind, where anxiety always resided. Is it possible I have found a lifeline through this nightmare? I sure hope so.

For all our sakes.

The Only Ones Left is the debut novel of K.E. Jennings.

This and two other psychological thrillers by this exciting new author are available via Amazon and selected retailers worldwide.

Christmas Past

By Jane Murray

'I can't believe it's December 24th already,' Esme sighed, and moved away from the window, trotting back to her workstation before she was spotted, and beaten for wasting time. She sat down on the uncomfortable black stool and stretched her back, before tucking herself in again and turning her eyes back to the screen.

Her colleague, Daz, shrugged. 'So what?' he said, not taking his eyes of his screen, afraid that he might miss something vital. 'This time of year is miserable, relentless. 'They' say all the extra transactions are a throwback to days gone by, when they celebrated something called 'Christmas.' Daz cocked his head over to the group of Elders clustered around the unit's entrance door to indicate who he was alluding to.

Esme nodded, busy tracking someone as they were in the process of paying for their monthly grocery shopping. Upon checking their Social Score, Esme clicked a button. 'Payment Denied.' They hadn't reached the required Social Score status to spend that much Electrocoin. What they did and how they explained it to the storekeeper was not Esme's concern. The family would start the next month with a black mark, meaning their Social Score was immediately reduced by five Credits. They probably wouldn't be able to buy next month's shopping, either. But that wasn't Esme's problem.

'I've heard about Christmas,' she sighed, clearing her screen, and accepting another transaction. 'It sounds nice.'

'Well, it would be nicer than having two extra shifts to do here today and tomorrow,' Daz replied. Then he looked guilty. 'My Social isn't exactly exemplary this month.'

Esme glanced at him and authorised two other transactions swiftly lest one of the Elder's reprimanded her for talking. She did not want her Social Score to be black marked.

'Yes, well, I did warn you what socialising does for your score. How many black marks did you get for going to the pub during the week?'

Daz looked rueful. 'Two, so I'm down ten Credits. But I'm working extra to make up for it, and that should please you – know – who.' He nodded again at the Elders and received a sharp look from his Manager Elder. It put paid to any further conversation for the rest of a rather bleak afternoon.

Outside, the sky was a dull, leaden colour and low-lying clouds scudded across the horizon as if they were rushing off somewhere. There was a mean wind, which whipped at your collar and lashed at your face with harsh, cold blasts.

'I wonder if the weather was the same in the olden days?' mused Daz, as he and Esme climbed up the hill to wait for their Social Transport back to their Housing Unit. It was the end of their shift, and they were both tired. Their eyes were sore from staring at their screens for ten hours. Once they got back to their Housing Unit, they would just have time to wash and change for dinner before maybe having an hour of Recreation before Lights Out.

Esme shivered and stamped her feet, which were turning into blocks of ice. 'Well, it couldn't have been any worse than this,' she replied. 'It's awful. I hope they have got some heating on in the unit, otherwise, I'm skipping dinner and going to bed.'

Daz nodded bleakly. 'God, yes. Same for me, and I have to be up earlier than you, anyway, as I'm doing an extra shift tomorrow. It would be Christmas Day, in the olden times.'

Their Social Transport arrived, and they didn't talk once they'd settled themselves inside the shared electronic, unmanned vehicle. There were several other passengers, and they didn't know any of them. Careless talk still cost lives, after the pandemics and the Reset. But Esme took up the subject of Christmas again once they disembarked and were heading towards their Housing Unit, a squat, two storey utilitarian building that did little to please the eye or enhance the landscape.

'How come you know so much about Christmas, Daz?' she asked, puffing slightly as they walked up the steep hill which led 'home', although there wasn't anything remotely homely about living there, she thought. She sometimes remembered what it was like, when she'd lived with her parents as children were allowed to do until they were thirteen and considered eligible for work in addition to their education, which Esme had completed, now that she was sixteen. After that, you worked full time, until you were eligible for selection to be parented. Then, she would become someone's Helpmate, and eventually, a mother. She would be allowed to have one child and after that, once parenting was complete and the child turned thirteen, she and her partner would return to life within another Housing Unit, where they would work until they were put to sleep. She didn't like the idea of being forced to sleep. It didn't seem fair, but then, not a lot in life was. Her only hope was to be recognised at work for her industry, and then she might be made an Elite, if she had amassed enough Social Credits.

'I talk to my grandfather,' Daz told her, bringing her thoughts back to where she and Daz had just reached the Housing Unit and would have to go through security, just as they did every night.

'Is that wise?' she whispered, as they were scanned and given permission to pass through the metal barrier which would give them access to what they called 'home.'

'No, probably not,' replied Daz, who knew the rules as well as she did, but was better at breaking them. 'But it is more comforting than this.' He gestured around the long, empty corridor, painted a sickly beige. The floors were concrete and each side of the corridor there were numbered Pod doorways. This was where they lived. She shared a pod with two other girls. There was always three to a pod, because two, after all, is company, but three, is definitely a crowd.

'Why don't you come with me tonight?' asked Daz, his dark brown, almost black eyes shining in the harsh overhead light.

'I daren't! What about the others in my pod?'

'Do what I do, promise them a credit. Honestly, Esme, they'll do it. Most people will do anything for spare credits. Come on, Grandfather will cheer you up, I promise.'

Suddenly Esme was assailed with a loneliness she'd never given much thought to before. Always the 'good' girl, she did as she was told, went to work, saved her credits, and had plenty of complimentary reports on her work and general attitude to life. Well, tonight, her attitude to life included throwing caution to the wind and going to visit Daz's grandfather!

'I'll meet you straight after supper,' she told him, with a tinge of excitement in her voice.

Daz's grandfather was an Elder, given the status because of his exemplary work record – he still worked now at eighty, having avoided being put to sleep fifteen years ago on the basis of his usefulness to society. He was an extraordinary human being – the eldest person alive in this Domain, anyway.

'Oh, 'ello, Esme love,' he said now, his voice amazingly still bore a trace of an accent from a place once known as Lancashire, where the old man had been born. The Reset and everything that had happened in the recent past to bring them to the present day seemed not to have had any impact on Eli Binks.

'Hello, Mr. Binks,' Esme smiled, a bit nervously, for being in Eli's presence had that effect on most people, except for Daz, and his parents.

'Sit th'yself down, young Esme, lass,' said the old man now, pulling up a chair towards the fire – another luxury accorded to him because of his wisdom and great age – he lived alone in a small cottage on the edge of the Domain. This, thought Esme, as she did as Eli had bid and sat down on the wooden framed lounge chair that he had indicated; this was a real home. The pods, she decided, were not 'home', they were just somewhere to live.

'Granddad,' Daz gave the old man's arm a playful punch and received a scuff around the neck and a ruffling of his spiky hair in return, 'tell us about Christmas. Esme doesn't really believe it existed, but you know, don't you? You're old enough to remember when today was – what did you call it the other day? Christmas Eve?'

'Oh, aye, I do, that, lad. Yes, Christmas did exist, Esme love, and right good it were, too. Not like nowadays, everyone's either forgotten about it or they're too scared to remember it!' The indignation in his voice was palpable.

He leaned forwards to the two youngsters, wanting them to get closer to share the magic with him. His words filled the room, and Esme felt her surroundings getting warmer, the light became softer, and she could smell a strange and exotic, almost a woodland smell.

The cottage where Eli Binks lived now, was the cottage Eli had lived in since the day he was born. Time warped and weft, people had been born in this cottage and people had died there. Prayers for the deceased had been sung, births and marriages celebrated and every year, the tiny little stone-built room took on a magical appearance.

Esme gasped and stared around her. The huge fireplace, with the glowing amber of the flames reflecting back at her, was swathed in garlands of greenery, with bright red berries. Huge, fat ribbons were tied in bows at either end and in the centre of the fireplace, above which, on the mantel, were coloured candles, with dancing flames and enticing smells. Beneath her feet was a thick, sheepskin rug, which she could swear wasn't there before. A basket stuffed full of thick, aromatic logs and twigs sat on the hearth next to a delicately and intricately carved reindeer. Esme wanted to reach out and touch it but did not dare. She wasn't sure if it was real or not, anyway.

She could hear Eli's voice in the background, describing everything she could see. He pointed behind him, to the far corner of the room and there, as he promised, was a tall, fat Christmas tree, resplendent with coloured baubles, candy canes, fir cones and tinsel. Strings of pretty, coloured lights were tangled up between the branches, and they twinkled in the semi darkness.

'Take a deep breath, lass,' smiled Eli. 'Sniff up!'

She sniffed. The most mouth-watering smell of cooking

greeted her small, snub nose. Rich, warm, and spicy. She licked her lips and glanced beyond the staircase to a small open door; beyond it, she espied a kitchen. A halo of light and activity, she could see a woman, wearing a white apron, dashing from oven to counter, raising her hand, basting a huge joint of meat before placing it back in the large cooker. Steam rose from several pans on the hob. Swathes of tinsel were looped beneath the wall mounted cabinets and there was the sound of music, rhythmic, lilting, coming from a small box on the table by the door.

'Aye, we always used to listen t'radio on Christmas Eve. Nice, isn't it, the Christmas music. Carols, they called them. They were hymns we sung at Christmas time, to celebrate the birth of Jesus Christ, our Lord, although no-one believes in him nowadays. Even thirty or forty years ago, people still believed, but they're all gone, now and you can't forget something you were never told about. So, none of your generation even know our Lord. The Elders wouldn't teach you – goes against everything they believe in since the Reset. But ah still believe, in me own way, here. I still sing the hymns to mesel' an' I still praise God at Christmas.'

Eli's voice petered out into the cosy darkness of the room, and suddenly, Esme became aware of singing – it was coming from outside, she thought, looking around in wonderment to see if anyone else had heard it, too.

Eli nodded. 'Carol singers, Esme, love. Every Christmas Eve they used to call here. Ours was the last house before the Church, so they'd end here, and we'd give them mince pies and hot mulled wine before we all headed up to Church for the celebrations. Open the door, lass, see for yourself.'

Esme did as she was bid, and opened the heavy, wooden door to the cottage, aware of Daz behind her and both children gasped in awe at the sight of the group of people outside, all clad in thick, warm clothing, hats, and mittens. They had bright red cheeks from the cold and they stamped their feet. But then, they forgot about the cold, and began to sing and for the first time in her life, Esme heard the haunting and melodic refrain of 'Silent Night'. She was transfixed and if Daz hadn't nudged her, she wouldn't have looked up into the night sky to see the fat, floating snowflakes cascading down, haphazard, beautiful, icy flakes.

'Aye, we had many a white Christmas here, we did, in the olden days. I stood at that door every Christmas Eve listening to the carol singers, and happen as not, it would be snowing. Close t'door now, Esme, love, keep the warmth in. They'll carry on singing for a while out there.'

Closing the door, ears straining to hear the carols, Esme turned back into the living room, and watched, transfixed as the woman wearing the apron came into the room and pulled up a large table, upon which she placed the most delightful array of tiny pastries, things Esme did not recognise, but which she knew from the smell, were delicious.

'And every Christmas Eve, we would have a little supper of sausage rolls, pork pies – the gelatine oozing out of them – tiny little cubes of cheese and the littlest onions on sticks, and of course, the mince pies and Christmas shortbread. Oh, what a treat the Christmas supper was. We'd wash it all down with the mulled wine, and we'd always ask the carol singers in when they had finished the last hymn. We knew it was the last hymn when they sand 'Away in a Manger.'

Eli's eyes seemed moist as he remembered the days of his youth, when he had been the strapping young lad that his grandson, Daz, now was. In his minds' eye he could see his Edie, a buxom young girl, eager and in love with him. They both sat on the floor, like these two kids were doing now, tucking into the repast his mother had made for them. Now, every Christmas, Edie would still make their supper, and they would still listen to the sound of the carollers, singing their hymns before they went to Church.

'Are you coming, or what?' asked Daz, impatiently. 'I'm bloody freezing here.'

Esme shook her head and looked around in disbelief. Where was the cottage, and Eli? Where were the beautiful decorations and the Christmas tree, and the sound of the carol singers, still resonating in Esme's head?

Looking around in a slight panic, Esme grabbed hold of Daz, who looked surprised and then concerned.

'What's the matter, Esme? You look funny.'

'Daz, where's the cottage, and your granddad? He was here, or we were there, and he was telling us all about Christmas. It was beautiful. There were mince pies and carol singers and the cottage looked lovely, with all the Christmas decorations.' Esme's eyes shone with the memory.

Daz shook his head. 'I don't know what you're going on about, Esme, but I know we'll get into trouble if we miss Social Transport back to the Unit. Come on, hurry up!'

He grabbed hold of her sleeve and started to pull her uphill, towards the designated stop for the Social Transport vehicle. She sighed. It had all been a daydream, she thought, unhappily. Just a silly daydream.

There were several other people waiting for the vehicle to arrive, so Daz and Esme lingered a little at the back, so that they got the seats closest to the front, which they loved. As the vehicle pulled to a halt, and everyone jostled to board and get their preferred seats, Esme cast a glance around, wishing she could see the cottage again and feel its welcoming warmth. How lucky people had been, back then, before the Reset, she thought. Christmas was obviously a time of celebration and joy. She remembered the tree, in the corner of the cottage's cosy living room and the parcels wrapped in shiny paper by its side.

Throughout the journey, she didn't speak, and Daz kept shooting her concerned glances. Back at her pod, she laid in her small bunk, not bothering to go to tea, preferring to tuck herself up with her beautiful Christmas daydream, which she played over and over in her head until finally, she fell asleep.

The next morning dawned crisp and bright, with a sharp coldness in the air. She was awakened by the horn, as usual and along with the others in the pod, she washed and dressed, made her bed, and tidied up, in case they had an inspection. Then, it was breakfast time. The others rushed her out, before she realised, she'd forgotten her digital pass-card. She wouldn't be allowed to the refectory without it, or out of the building. Making apologies and telling the others to go on ahead, Esme retraced her footsteps back to the pod.

There was no inspection, so she was quite alone in the sudden stillness. She went into the sleeping quarters, and there, on her bed, to her amazement, sat a shiny, wrapped parcel and a mince pie.

'Merry Christmas, lass,' said Eli, as she spun around in wonder. 'Merry Christmas from the past.'

This short story was first published in a previous compilation – A Cosy Christmas – which is also available from Provoco Publishing.

Subservient

By Christopher Grumley

The city sprawled haphazardly across the landscape. Modera, like all the cities of Cepheon, buzzed with boisterous activity. Teelo Mar sat under the canopy of a tree, listening to the language of the city, the ion drives of shuttles that interweaved its tall stone and steel buildings, the bodiless voices of thousands upon thousands of voices meshing into one. Even at midday, the neon lights of the inner city and vast advertisements twinkled like a million jewels in the gloom of an immense platform above—the sky city of Calvera overhead.

A distant roar sounded from the heart of the city. His eyes darted first towards the noise, then to a column of blue glass which towered skywards from the city and up into the base of the Calvera platform. It was decorated in an ornate helical lattice of intertwining metal and was known to everyone as the Tract. A faint dot emerged inside the Tract. It travelled smoothly down, disappearing into the white domed roof of a building known as the Junction to the Cerebrals, but the Subservients knew it only as the Barrier—the barrier which separated the Cerebrals above from the Subservients on the ground. The roar sounded again but carried a tinge of anger and hate this time. At that moment, he realised that the city of Modera had settled into its usual Unity Day routine: hate, protests and violence.

Pressing himself back, he turned from the city and drifted briefly, then peered off the cliff edge to the ocean-drenched rocks below. Waves crashed and roared, lifting spray into the air, tantalising his nostrils with a pleasant sea breeze.

Teelo sat up, drew his knees to his chest and hugged them. For a moment, sadness overcame him. His heart fluttered as a memory came to mind—when he had brought his wife, Reti, here. It was her favourite place. But now he knew she would never see it again; her health was failing, her hypnogogic death approaching. He turned his head back to the city, his stomach sick with the nausea of forgotten happiness. He cast his green eyes up one of the vast struts of the sky city towards Calvera, hardly visible within looming clouds burdened with heavy rain.

Teelo watched as monstrous automated cannons with laser eyes tracked cruisers and shuttles as they approached the platform. No one from the ground ever made it to Calvera, and it filled him with resentment, thinking that someone up there might be able to save his beloved Reti.

A rumble of deep thunder rolled through the surrounding hills as he glared. He looked skyward, and a black dot grew on the horizon as he did. It was coming straight towards him.

Thrusting his muscular frame up, he stepped out from under the tree to the cliff edge, then focused and strained his eyes. A military-spec shuttle, a personnel carrier, came closer and closer with each moment. Soon, it skimmed by overhead, churning the air and sending him tumbling. He wiped the strands of long brown hair from his face, dusted his hands on his filthy miner's overalls and raced back down the hill towards Mining Facility Four.

Nearing the compound, a maelstrom of Subservients swelled like a wave and crashed upon a wall of soldiers. The Neutros, their bodies covered head to toe in a second skin of white nanoparticle plate armour, forced them back, holding them at gunpoint.

He dashed through a security gate and into the compound. A cold wind swirled through the complex as the rain began to fall. Large droplets exploded off the plate armour with a tinny quality. Behind them, the harsh crack of a whip ripped the air. And agonised screams echoed around the compound.

He scythed his way through the crowd and stared momentarily at the ghostly blue faces of the soldiers, their mouths and chins washed in blue from light sneaking out from below the impenetrable black visor strip of their helmets.

Beyond, he caught a glimpse of a Subservient—a Fledgling—chained to a metal post, his shirt torn and blood pouring from slashes across his back. The thick-set frame of Commander Pasha stood back a short distance, his drenched silvery hair flailing in the wind as he grunted and released each thunderous blow.

The chained Subservient fell quiet, and the commander squelched forward across the gravelled ground.

'Wake up!' barked the commander, spitting rain from his lips as he spoke. He launched a heavy barrage of kicks at the man's abdomen, grasped his cheeks and slapped him back to consciousness. 'You don't get a free ride. I want you to feel everything.'

Several more blows struck. The man screamed and broke down in tears. Spittle flew from the Subservient's mouth with each crushing blow.

'Damn.' A voice he recognised. He turned and looked to his left and saw the familiar ageless faces of his friends Lou, Berin, Cayo and Jarro. Teelo shouldered through the crowd towards them.

'What's happened?' asked Teelo.

Screams. Agonised cries. Teelo winced, as did the others.

'Not sure,' said Jarro in a husky voice, 'But it ain't looking good for that Fledger.' The concern in his silver-white eyes was apparent. The two shorter men behind Jarro jostled for a view.

'We were in Section B when this all started,' said the younger man, Berin. The rain, driving in slanted, sent black rivers of soot streaming from his face, revealing his olive skin.

'No announcement, either!' barked Lou, his curled red-brown hair peeking beneath his protective helmet. 'These Neutros, man. They're messed up. Beatin' a Fledger. I swear more and more of these new-borns are bein' brought in each week and being carted out in med-evacs before they even get down the mines.'

'Aye, and you boys keep yer heads down, else that'll be you, too,' growled the older and somewhat wiser Cayo. Rain streaked off his filth-heavy moustache. 'Yous watch and know yer place. Don't go getting involved, ya hear?'

The Fledger lay on the ground, shaking as the Commander kicked at his ribs relentlessly.

'But Cayo, look what's happenin'!' grunted Berin, gesturing a strong arm.

A thunderous, wet slap of flesh caught their attention. Teelo and Jarro recoiled. Lou and Berin stood mouth agape as the violence ensued. Cayo watched with a fixed stare, a figure of measured calm.

Pasha, panting heavily and baring his teeth, broke from his attack and circled. Bloodied water dripped from the thong of his whip. He bellowed at the statue-like crowd.

'How many times do I need to tell you? Insubordination will not be tolerated!' He turned back and paced forward towards the man, his whip ready. All the miners watched on in dread. The Neutros tensed their fingers on their autorifles. And guards in the perimeter watch towers swivelled their turrets and readied.

Strength filled his body as his heart swelled with confidence; his eyes narrowed, and fists readied. Feeling courage he had not known grow within him, he barged forward, shedding Cayo's grasp and past the line of Neutros.

'Stop this!' he cried. 'You wanna fight somebody? You can come and fight me!' He raised his fists above his head, and his stance widened.

Pasha turned, stunting a laugh and ordering the Neutros to lower their weapons with a dismissive flick of his hand.

'And… who are you?' grumbled Pasha.

'Teelo Mar. Leave the man alone. He's done. If you want more blood, I've got plenty.' Teelo loosened his shoulders and began to move slowly in the opposite direction to the commander.

Pasha gave him a piercing look and then lashed a crack of his whip. Teelo felt the sharp sting of leather slice through the skin at the top of his arm. He recoiled in agony and fell to the ground as his unharmed hand grasped his wounded arm tightly. His legs withdrew into his chest, coiling as he rolled about the floor. Not a sound could be heard save for the howling of the wind, the hiss of the rain as it leapt off the ground and Teelo's anguished cries.

When the pain had subsided, he removed his hand to find his palm-stained bright red. Blood gushed from a sizable wound. Pasha turned back to his prisoner tied against the post when Teelo rose defiantly to his feet with a grimace.

'You've got balls. But that'll only get you so far with me. Move back!' exclaimed Pasha, 'Or I'll string you up alongside this one.'

'No!' replied Teelo as he stood in a pained stagger, his arms weakened by the weight of his soaked clothes. 'I won't let you do this. The man is broken – leave him be.'

Pasha paused for a moment in stunned silence. The rain hammered down like millions of cold daggers across his face; his hair swept about in the prevailing winds. His hand tightened about the whip as he clenched his teeth in a belligerent grimace. With a menace, he threw his whip and barrelled towards Teelo, his breath deepening as anger grew.

Teelo stood stoically, fists raised in anticipation of the crashing wave of wrath about to be unleashed upon him.

Suddenly, a flash seared through the clouds above. In the blinding light, Pasha emerged and began to unleash a bombardment of face-bound white-knuckle blows. Teelo raised his forearms and slipped to the side. Pasha flailed an elbow that missed his head. In an instant, Teelo wrapped his arms around Pasha's neck from behind and squeezed.

The pair struggled as the cold sheets of rain descended on them – another flash of light with a boom and crack.

Pasha broke powerfully through Teelo's grip with a sharp backwards flick of his head and a stinging elbow to his midriff. Teelo stumbled down on one knee, clutching his stomach.

Another thunderous flash lit the sky.

As Teelo crouched in recoiled pain, time appeared to slow down. The ice-cold rain traced paths across his face, mixing with the warmth of his blood as it trailed down his nose.

A boom and a crash; light forking.

Out of the white flash appeared two heavy fists. Teelo fell to his back. A daze took him, and he drifted into a moment of memory.

Teelo floats in a vessel of lurid green amniotic fluid. It is cold and stings his skin. His muscular arms float. He feels something. Looking down at a fully grown and ageless body, black tubes penetrate him...

'Nutrient lines,' says the fuzzy faces beyond the glass.

Teelo feels his heart race...

Weak fists slam the glass. A black rebreather smothering his face stifles his screams... his heart beats... faster... faster... faster.

The faces get closer. There are three of them—men in white coats.

'Batch one-seven-three-eight-six designation-C ready for Fledging. Commence.'

The green soup flushes. It is so cold. The lines explode from his skin. Blood oozes. Fear grips him. Light erupts. Dripping water fills his ears. The rebreather snaps away, and the glass door swings open. The impact with the ground sears pain through his body. He gasps, and air floods his lungs... burning... burning... burning...

Taking advantage, Pasha launched forward and mounted his foe. Left, right – his fists found their target – left, right again. Teelo's mind drifted once more.

Reti sits on a hill. On a blanket. The wind carries her fragrance and excites his nose.

Water roars... rocks sizzle far below.

The shoreline... it is beautiful, he thinks, but not as beautiful as you.

He strokes golden strands of hair off her exposed shoulder. Her skin excites his lips, and he moves to her neck. Her body responds to his touch.

Reti turns.

'Teelo, I love you.'

A surge of adrenaline coursed along Teelo's nervous system, returning him to his senses. A fist flew at his head. He thrust an arm upward into the commander's chest, holding him while his other hand fumbled blindly for anything, stopping when they felt something hard.

A stone.

Teelo's fingers crawled over it like an insect, grasped it tight. He swung his arm, but the commander saw the blow coming, ducked and spun away on his knees.

Dazed, Teelo staggered to his feet, licking away the metallic taste of blood-mingled rain from his lips.

Pasha moved slowly and measured his opponent, waiting for an opening. Teelo, his vision fuzzing at the edges, stumbled forward and swung lazily, missing by some distance. Pasha side-stepped, thrust a knee into Teelo's abdomen, then crunched his face with a fist.

Teelo fell to the ground, his head grating in the soddened gravel. He lay half-submerged in a puddle as his consciousness drifted once more.

Darkness. Death lingers in the air.

'I'm dying, Teelo, I'm dy—' Reti begins.

'Ssh,' interjects Teelo.

He presses her hand against his cheek. Once, it had been soft and delicate, now... a skeletal claw. Lifting her legs, he swaddles her with the duvet and rolls her onto her side.

She coughs uncontrollably as he does, gasping for air.

Panic fills him. Medicines... he cannot find the medicines. Quickly... quickly... He races through the apartment to the bedroom and finds an actuator. Fumbling, he loads it and rushes back.

Reti gasps. No air enters her lungs. She is blue.

He thrusts the actuator into her mouth and triggers it. Her breath eases, dimming to a low wheeze as she drifts into a deep sleep.

Reti's arm droops off the side of the couch. A serial number. A date. Her hypnogogic death date... is near.

Teelo places a hand on his chest. His heart calms. He stands and moves to the window and looks out. The horizon lights up with electricity. He turns his eyes to his arm, at his serial number, and a date three years and six months from now.

All the Subservients watched in dismay – the repeated thud of fists intermingled with the crashing light above. Teelo was slipping in and out of consciousness, but the pounding continued. Without an instant for thought, Lou sprang forward with haste. Running like fire, he sped over to the scene.

'Stop!' screamed Lou, his arms outstretched, despair and anguish heavy in his voice. 'Please stop – you're killing him.'

Pasha restrained and turned towards Lou, regarding him with a piercing glance. Suddenly, he stood, his hands balled. The fire and malice in his gaze caused Lou to step back. The Commander clenched his jaw as he bared his teeth; with a harsh breath, he strode with furious intent towards Lou. One hand wrapped around the grip of his pistol as the other, thrust outwards, grasped Lou's shirt and pulled him close, the gun barrel pressed against his temple. Lou threw his arms up in surrender. All in the courtyard stood paralysed in silence.

'I will stop when this fool learns his lesson,' said Pasha. 'He interfered with justice, and I will decide when the punishment has been served.'

'I never said he was clever,' replied Lou. 'You're right – he intervened. But he's done... look at him.' Lou nodded towards Teelo on the floor.

Pasha scowled downwards, eyeing Teelo's bludgeoned face and grunted. His gaze returned to Lou and met his warm, brown eyes. 'Please – his wife is dying. She's near hypno. He's all she's got. Don't kill him here and leave her alone; she ain't got long left.' Pasha pondered, the gears of his mind turning as the pitter-patter of rain cut through the silence. A slight grin broke across his face as his eyebrows danced disapprovingly.

'Alright,' he said as he holstered his weapon. He released his grip on Lou, who expelled a sigh of relief. 'Okay. But next time...' Pasha stepped forward in confrontation '... It won't be a fight. It'll be a bullet.' Lou gave a reluctant nod as he retreated. Pasha turned in a slow circle.

'Clear the compound!' bellowed Pasha in his commanding voice. At once, all those in the courtyard scampered and scuttled in haste towards the main entrance. Jarro, Berin and Cayo ran towards where Lou was tending to Teelo, who lay barely awake and muttering incoherent words.

'Quick, guys,' said Lou with urgency. 'Quick…let's get him to the infirmary.' Each grasped a limb and proceeded with care across the soggy ground. They slipped and slid towards a small weather-beaten stone building and burst through the steel doors. Once inside, they placed Teelo gently on a trolley. There he lay, staring into the lights on the ceiling above. Around him, sounds faded to an incoherent mumble, and his world closed on him in a haze. Then, Teelo felt himself falling, and confusion seemed to rise and engulf him. He didn't hear or see anything as he fell into a deep sleep.

Subservient is the debut novel from sci-fi fantasy author, Christopher Grumley and will be available mid-2026.

About the Authors

Christopher Grumley

 Chris is a qualified dentist working as a Dental Core Trainee in the West of Scotland. He graduated from the University of Glasgow in 2022 with a Bachelor of Dental Surgery with Honors (BDS Hons), but his professional journey didn't start there. Before diving into the world of dentistry, Chris was a registered pharmacist, a role he dedicated nearly a decade of his life to. This background in pharmacy has given him a well-rounded perspective on patient care, one that he carries into his dental practice today.

Chris's career in healthcare is not the only facet of his life. He is also a passionate reader, particularly of fantasy and science fiction novels. This love for imaginative storytelling took on a new dimension during the COVID-19 pandemic. With the gift of extra time, Chris decided to channel his creativity into writing. In 2020, he embarked on a journey of crafting science fiction dystopian novels, with a special focus on cyberpunk aesthetics. His writing, influenced by the fantastical worlds he loves to read about, is a testament to his resilience and creativity during challenging times.

But Chris's life is not all about work and writing. He is an adventurer at heart. His hobbies reflect his love for the great outdoors—hill walking, camping, and developing outdoorsman skills. These activities not only provide a physical challenge but also offer a refreshing break from his professional responsibilities. The tranquillity of nature and the thrill of adventure fuel his creative processes, providing inspiration for the dystopian worlds he builds in his novels.

When he's not lost in the wilderness or the pages of a book, Chris values the time spent with his friends and family. These moments of connection and relaxation are essential to him, providing a balance to his busy life. He understands the importance of these relationships and how they ground him, giving him the support needed to pursue his varied interests.

Sports are another passion for Chris. He is an avid Formula 1 fan, captivated by the speed, strategy, and skill involved in the races. Additionally, his unwavering support for Everton Football Club adds another layer to his profile. Despite the team's ups and downs, Chris remains a hopeful and dedicated fan, eagerly anticipating a trophy in the near future. This loyalty and optimism are traits that resonate in his personal and professional life.

Chris's journey is one of balancing multiple passions. His transition from pharmacy to dentistry showcases his dedication to healthcare, while his foray into writing highlights his creative side. This blend of science and art, of practicality and imagination, makes him a relatable and grounded individual. He doesn't see himself as someone extraordinary but as someone who follows his interests and seeks fulfilment in various aspects of life. His writing, particularly in the science fiction dystopian genre, is where many of his interests converge. The cyberpunk aesthetics reflect his fascination with the future and technology, while the dystopian themes often mirror the challenges and complexities he encounters in the real world. Through his novels, Chris invites readers to explore these intricate worlds with him, offering not just escapism but also thought-provoking narratives.

In essence, Chris is a testament to the idea that you can pursue multiple passions and still find balance. Whether he's in the dental clinic, out in nature, or at his writing desk, he brings a sense of curiosity and dedication to everything he does. His story is one of following your passions, finding balance, and remaining hopeful and grounded, no matter where your journey takes you.

John Howard

 John lives in Blackpool and not surprisingly, given the mentions of the silver screen and boxing in John's debut novel, he loves the cinema and boxing!

When he's not writing, or working, John helps his wife bring up their daughter, Daisy-Mae and supporting Everton Football Club, who he says need all the help they can get!

John is currently writing the second book in The Crawford Chronicles, due for publication in mid-2026. The first book in this ambitious series, A Scandal of Secrets was released in 2023 and begins a roller coaster ride through the echelons of high society in 1920's England. The series will culminate at the start of the 2000's.

Having crossed the divide between writing as a journalist and writing as a novelist, John continues to develop his author repertoire with a children's book planned in collaboration with his daughter, Daisy – Mae.

John's debut novel, A Scandal of Secrets is currently available.

Dawn Treacher

Dawn Treacher joined Provoco in 2023, when she published her debut cosy crime novel, The Seeds of Murder with us. This was Dawn's first novel for a grown-up audience.

Dawn is an established children's book author and illustrator. Her love of crime fiction has seen her embark on a new series of cosy crime mysteries, fuelled by her love of amateur sleuths, gardening, and inspired by the rural North Yorkshire villages in which she has lived over the last twenty years.

In the warmer months she can be found writing in Geraldine, her caravan in the garden. As a carer for her husband, writing has long been her creative outlet in which she supports fellow writers to master, by running creative writing and critique groups.

Dawn has just published her third novel with Provoco, and we are pleased that two others are already in the pipeline, the first of which is publishing in early 2026 and will be Dawn's first foray into psychological thriller writing!

Dawn's three novels, The Seeds of Murder, A Deadly Plot and The Ninth Life of Norris are all available published by Provoco.

Nicholas Vaughan

 Nicholas Vaughan is an artist with a varied practice from sculpture to drawing, mixed media to installation, often developing fictional texts for the illustration of his artwork. He received his degree in Sculpture from Wolverhampton University (2001) and an MA in Fine Art from Chelsea College of Art and Design (2002).

His work has been shown in shows throughout Europe, including at The

Corner House Gallery in Manchester and Imperial College in London as well as at Gliwice Museum in Poland. He has work in public and private collections.

Provoco is delighted to have been approached by Nicholas to publish his latest book (he has two self-published novels already released), which he tells us was a labour of love, and which kept him busy and amused during lockdown! Nicholas is in the process of writing further work for Provoco about climate change and the environment.

Nicholas' debut novel for Provoco, The Unwrapping, was released in October 2025 and we eagerly await the next!

A.H. Martin

Andy H Martin has been writing short stories for the past eight years and has recently finished his first novel.

He was born in the south of England. His love of travel began at the tender age of six when his father took up a post as chief engineer at an industrial diamond mine Ghana. As a teenager he spent several summers traveling across Europe.

Andy trained as a Radiographer at St George's Hospital, London, qualifying in 1977. He worked in various hospitals in England and the Middle East for the following 22 years. His last clinical position was as Head Radiographer at a major international Cardiovascular hospital in Saudi Arabia.

His roles included designing and developing new interventional Cardiovascular imaging systems for Philips and devising the training procedures for hospital staff and application specialists. He travelled extensively, supporting the introduction of these new systems into the different regions of the world. Training clinicians, staff and the local application specialists, and troubleshooting IQ issues. Andy and his family then moved to the Netherlands in 1999 where he spend the next 20 years working for Philips Healthcare as a senior clinical application specialist. In 2019, he retired after 40 years involved in differing aspects of medical X-Ray imaging.

Andy now enjoys his retirement on a 64ft replica Dutch Barge cruising the canals and rivers of western Europe and indulging his love of writing.

A.H. Martin's debut novel, Living Proof, the first in a trilogy of crime thrillers, is now available on Amazon and in selected retailers.

Carol Leyland

 In addition to writing, Carol is an historian and archaeologist. She earned her BA and MA in Historical Archaeology from the University of York in her early 50s. She has a particular interest in the 19th century, focusing on workhouses and asylums, as well as the biographies of the women and children who lived in those oppressive and frightening institutions.

She grew up in York, where she has lived for most of her life. Her books are inspired by the areas from her childhood and the places she has worked. Over the years, she has held a variety of jobs, including Editor-in-Chief of the Archaeology journal at the University of York, rare-breed sheep farmer, home carer, administrator, and charity worker.

Carol writes short stories for Provoco and has previously self-published two novels.

Emma Hardy

 Emma Hardy is originally from Cornwall but now lives in South Wales. Civil servant by day and active imagination user by night, Emma has recently joined Provoco on a three-book deal.

A book lover since the age of four when her Pops took her to get her first library card, Emma has been championing books ever since. She is a book blogger found on social media @bobsandbooks.

Emma has had many short stories published by Provoco Publishing, and Caab Publishing. Her ambition is to tell real stories of forgotten women, whilst holding a mirror to modern society. Emma's debut novel for Provoco is due for publication in early 2026.

Jane Murray

 Jane Murray is a multi-genre author who writes under her own name and under the pseudonym of D.C. Cummings. Her work ranges from historical supernatural tales to chick lit to psychological thrillers and her first foray into this particular genre, written as D.C. Cummings, was released in October 2025 and more books in this genre are planned. Other forthcoming publications include a sequel to her debut novel, The Cottage, which is still Provoco Publishing's number one best seller, a cosy crime novella and a historical wartime family saga!

After a career in law, and jet setting around the world as part of her late partner's company that refurbished cruise liners, where she was Project Co-ordinator, Jane has now settled down to write in a four-hundred-year-old cottage on the English / Welsh borders. In January 2025, she suffered a life-threatening injury and two strokes, so she is extremely grateful both to the NHS, and God, for still be here and being able to write.

As the owner of Provoco Publishing, Jane is a strong proponent of independent publishing and will work with un-agented authors because she says it cuts out the middleman and leads to a better working relationship between author and publisher.

Jane lives alone but spends a lot of time being active in her village and church communities to stop her becoming a hermit, she says. In her spare time, she reads, walks and gardens, although not at the same time.

Ella Blackthorn

 We're delighted to have secured Ella Blackthorn on a three-book contract, the first of which, Finding Jack, is due to be released in 2026.

Ella has been previously published, but her next novel will be the first published by Provoco.

She has based the storyline of her novel in areas of the country that she loves and knows so well – Yorkshire and the Lake District. Ella was born in York.

Before becoming a novelist, Ella worked as a script writer for a television soap opera and has had some of her poetry previously published.

Her interests outside of writing include history, poetry and archaeology.

K.E. Jennings

Writing began as a hobby and morphed into a passion for KE Jennings. She loves crafting stories and characters that make you think, as well as showcasing the gritty side of life. The more realness, the better. Her favourite genre to write are thrillers that have a heart pounding flair.

She spent half of her childhood in the deserts of West Texas and the other in the mountains of Washington state. Quite the landscape difference, she learned to appreciate aspects of both, to include developing a lifelong love of the sea. KE learned to surf in the frigid waters of the Pacific Ocean, where she often longboarded and thankfully, never once saw a shark.

She served in the United States Army as an active-duty NCO for eight years as a Chaplain Assistant and was deployed for fifteen months to Iraq with a combat engineer battalion. While in the service, she lived in various locations to include Germany, Hawaii, and South Carolina. Her love of travel wasn't limited to her service though. She has taken trips to Australia, Austria, Mexico, Jamacia, St. Lucia, Canada, and all over the continental United States. Her favourite being Australia, because where else can you see kangaroos running wild?

After the Army, she obtained various college degrees in the healthcare field to include a Master's in Hospital Administration (MHA) and a master's in health systems management (M-HSM), as well as spending time volunteering at hospitals. Her other volunteer experience includes community outreach with local schools and with homeless programs run through her church.

In addition to writing, she is a self-professed outdoor fanatic and loves to fish, though worms make her squeamish. She loves hiking as well, preferring longer hikes that start after daybreak so the spider webs are already cleared off the trail by someone else's face. Avoiding bears and cougars the best she can, she likes the trails in the Cascade mountains as well as Mt. Rainier and surrounding areas. She also has a penchant for tacos and sunny weather, being Texas born.

You can find her at home with her family, out on a run, or cruising on her skateboard on a beachside trail. At the moment, she is working on various writing projects including some short stories. Katie's novels, The Only Ones Left, Bodies of Evidence and Key to Deception, can be found on Amazon and in selected retailers worldwide.

www.ingramcontent.com/pod-product-compliance
Lightning Source LLC
Chambersburg PA
CBHW051124260626
47170CB00005B/1658